"I look awful, don't I?" Pia asked.

"No. In fact—" Federico reached up to trace the outline of the white gauze "—you look wonderful for a woman who just had stitches." And he meant it. Most women would have fallen apart when told they'd face dozens of reporters after a day like hers. But not Pia.

"Well, if you think so, I'll take your word for it. But you have blood all over your shoulder."

Federico tried to reassure her. "I told you, I have other shirts. And perhaps it will not show on camera."

He bent down and dropped a soft kiss near her bandage. He intended it to be a quick peck, a confidence boost. But his lips lingered against her soft skin. His eyes closed as he savored the forbidden sensation of her curls brushing his face.

And in that moment, his carefully scheduled, precisely planned world came undone.

Dear Reader,

Whether our heroes are flirting with their best friends or taking care of adorable tots, their stories of falling for the right woman are sure to melt your heart. Don't miss one magical moment of this month's collection from Silhouette Romance.

Carolyn Zane begins THE BRUBAKER BRIDES miniseries by introducing us to the first of three Texas-bred sisters, in *Virginia's Getting Hitched* (SR #1730). Dr. Virginia Brubaker knows the secret to a long-lasting relationship: compatibility. But one sexy, irreverent ranch hand has a different theory all together…that he hopes to test on the prim but not-so-proper doctor!

In *Just Between Friends* (SR #1731), the latest emotion-packed tale from Julianna Morris, a handsome contractor rescues his well-to-do best friend by agreeing to marry her—for a year. But he doesn't know about her little white lie—for them, she's always wanted more than friendship.…

Prince Perfect always answers the call of duty…to his sons and to his kingdom. But his beautiful nanny tempts him to let go of his inhibitions and give in to the call of the heart. Find out if this bachelor dad will make the perfect husband, in *Falling for Prince Federico* (SR #1732) by Nicole Burnham.

The newest title from Holly Jacobs, *Be My Baby* (SR #1733), promises a rollicking good time! When a carefree single guy finds a baby on his doorstep, he's sure things couldn't get worse—until he's stranded in a snowstorm with his annoyingly attractive receptionist. With sparks flying, they're guaranteed to stay warm!

Sincerely,

Mavis C. Allen
Associate Senior Editor

Please address questions and book requests to:
Silhouette Reader Service
U.S.: 3010 Walden Ave., P.O. Box 1325, Buffalo, NY 14269
Canadian: P.O. Box 609, Fort Erie, Ont. L2A 5X3

Falling for
Prince Federico

NICOLE
BURNHAM

SILHOUETTE *Romance*®

Published by Silhouette Books

America's Publisher of Contemporary Romance

For the women who make me look good: Gail Chasan,
my incredible, kickin' editor; Jenny Bent, my very cool
and always stylish agent; and Emily Cotler, Web Diva
Extraordinaire. Thank you, thank you and thank you.

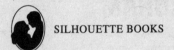 SILHOUETTE BOOKS

ISBN 0-373-19732-2

FALLING FOR PRINCE FEDERICO

Copyright © 2004 by Nicole Burnham Onsi

Visit Silhouette Books at www.eHarlequin.com

Printed in U.S.A.

Books by Nicole Burnham

Silhouette Romance

Going to the Castle #1563
The Prince's Tutor #1640
The Knight's Kiss #1663
One Bachelor To Go #1706
Falling for Prince Federico #1732

*The diTalora Royal Family

NICOLE BURNHAM

is originally from Colorado, but as the daughter of an army dentist grew up traveling the world. She has skied the Swiss Alps, snorkeled in the Grenadines and successfully haggled her way through Cairo's Khan al Khalili marketplace.

After obtaining both a law degree and a master's degree in political science, Nicole settled into what she thought would be a long, secure career as an attorney. That long, secure career only lasted a year—she soon found writing romance a more adventuresome career choice than writing stale legal briefs.

When she's not writing, Nicole enjoys relaxing with her family, tending her rose garden and traveling—the more exotic the locale, the better.

Nicole loves to hear from readers. You can reach her at P.O. Box 229, Hopkinton, MA, 01748-0229, or through her Web site at www.NicoleBurnham.com.

THE diTALORA FAMILY

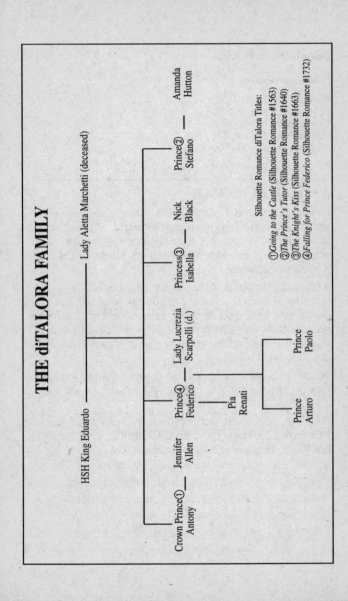

HSH King Eduardo — Lady Aletta Marchetti (deceased)

Crown Prince① Antony — Jennifer Allen

Prince④ Federico — Lady Lucrezia Scarpolli (d.)

Pia Renati

Prince Arturo

Prince Paolo

Princess③ Isabella — Nick Black

Prince② Stefano — Amanda Hutton

Silhouette Romance diTalora Titles:

① *Going to the Castle* (Silhouette Romance #1563)
② *The Prince's Tutor* (Silhouette Romance #1640)
③ *The Knight's Kiss* (Silhouette Romance #1663)
④ *Falling for Prince Federico* (Silhouette Romance #1732)

Chapter One

"I'm never going to be able to tell a placenta previa from a placenta accreta."

Pia Renati tried to keep her grumbling under her breath as she leaned one shoulder against the backlit cellular phone ad adorning the wall of the San Rimini International Airport and flipped to the next page of a thick, floral-jacketed pregnancy guide. How in the world did women have babies without a medical degree?

And why in the world had *she* gotten the call when her friend Jennifer Allen—now Princess Jennifer diTalora—needed someone to come stay with her during her obstetrician-imposed bed rest?

Pia's friends always looked to her in a disaster. As Pia's former boss at the refugee camp where they'd worked two years ago, Jennifer knew that better than anyone. Setting up food banks for refugees in third world nations came as naturally to Pia as walking. Helping to build temporary housing under a hot African sun? Transporting victims of war to medical facilities, or reuniting them with loved ones? Been there, done that. As a relief worker, Pia didn't fear hard work. But caring for a pregnant woman due to deliver the newest heir to San Rimini's throne at any time? What Pia knew about pregnancy and kids she'd learned in the last hour.

Her own mother hadn't exactly emulated Carol Brady or June Cleaver. Even Peg Bundy would have been an improvement over the perpetually-absent Sabrina Renati. At least Peg was home while she sat in front of the TV eating bonbons. But Jennifer insisted she wanted Pia by her side, and Pia wasn't about to say no to a pregnant princess.

Pia skipped to the next section of the pregnancy guide that Jennifer had sent her, nearly dropping it to the floor of the crowded airport terminal when faced with a full-page black-and-white photo of a woman giving birth. Couldn't these books leave anything to the imagination? Yeesh.

Well, she supposed it could have been in color.

"Signorina Renati?"

Pia barely heard the smooth baritone behind her, since at that exact moment the airport's public announcement system loudly requested that a Signor Ponizio pick up the white courtesy telephone.

Instead, a sudden sense of foreboding made Pia snap the book shut. The hum of conversation around her ceased and every single set of eyes on the concourse focused on the man behind her.

Without turning around, Pia realized who had to own the distinctive, opera-caliber voice. It wasn't a palace flunky as she'd expected, coming to show her the way to his Volkswagen minivan, but quite arguably the world's most desired single male, the recently widowed Prince Federico Constantin diTalora. The man known by tabloid readers everywhere as Prince Perfect for his Mediterranean good looks, unimpeachable reputation and his devotion to duty.

Of course. The one time she didn't get the chance to grab a breath mint or fix her makeup before getting off an overnight flight.

Hoping he hadn't been surveying her reading material over her shoulder, Pia forced herself to smile as she turned to face Jennifer's brother-in-law, the man second in line to the thousand-year-old throne of San Rimini.

Judging from the expression on his oft-photographed face, the prince had gotten a good look at the photo in the book.

It had been years since she'd been home and able to speak her native San Riminian-accented Italian, and Pia had been anxious to yak with someone who understood her heritage. Someone who could discuss San Riminian politics, give her the latest gossip about local celebrities, maybe rate the newest restaurants and dance clubs.

But the sight of the famous royal—a six-foot-two, well-toned man who filled out his understated black suit and crisp white shirt as well as any action star walking the red carpet at the Academy Awards—took her aback, and she only managed to get out a feeble, "Prince Federico. *Buon giorno. Come sta?*"

What in the world was he doing here? Jennifer never mentioned sending Federico to the airport. The dark-haired, blue-eyed prince not only towered over Pia, he possessed that intangible quality that every man coveted—charisma. When they'd been introduced during Jennifer's wedding to Crown Prince Antony nearly a year and a half ago, Pia had been so nervous she'd said the required niceties and quickly ducked back to the reception table where her co-workers from the Haffali refugee camp were seated, overwhelmed by the brief encounter.

Federico and his elegant wife—the late Princess Lucrezia—were polite enough, but both seemed above the festive, romantic atmosphere of the royal wedding. Lucrezia had been everything Pia wasn't—tall, rail-thin and pale, with dark, straight hair, full red lips and a cat-walk-worthy sense of style. The type of woman every fashion editor clamored to have featured in their magazines.

And Federico…well, his mere presence intimidated the hell out of her. His quiet, composed demeanor, combined with his polished shoes, custom-tailored tuxedo and royal sash had stolen her breath.

And then there were those amazing cheekbones. The

strong, smooth jaw that never showed a hint of five o'clock shadow. The even, olive-toned skin she imagined felt like heaven under a woman's fingertips.

Pia clasped the pregnancy book against her sage-green cotton T-shirt and wished she'd thought to dress a notch above khaki pants and athletic sandals. At least the last time she'd met Federico, she'd been wearing a poofy-but-respectable high-end bridesmaid's gown and designer heels.

The prince made a subtle gesture with his right hand, and a lean man standing nearby rushed forward to pick up the carry-on bag at Pia's feet. "I am quite well, Ms. Renati, thank you. However, if you do not mind, I would prefer to converse in English. I am attempting to improve my skills, and do not often get the chance to practice with someone who speaks both our language and English so well. You have spent a great deal of time in the United States, yes?"

She nodded. "English is fine." While she would have preferred Italian for casual conversation, having the prince call her signorina, as was customary in San Rimini, made her feel like a kid, and less mature than her thirty-two years. She held back a sigh. It wasn't as if he was the casual conversation type, anyway.

"Wonderful. I arranged for your suitcase to be delivered directly to the palace by the airline. Princess Jennifer is anxious to see you, so if you are ready to depart, my car is waiting through here." He indicated a set of thick metal doors along the concourse wall. To the right, through the floor-to-ceiling windows, Pia noticed a shiny black Mercedes limousine parked on the tarmac alongside the airplane from which she'd just disembarked.

The privilege of being a prince, she supposed. No need to battle for a parking spot, go through endless security checks, or wait for your suitcase alongside a hundred other tired travelers jockeying for position beside the baggage claim carousel.

The crowd parted in front of Federico as he led the way through the waiting area and out the gray metal doors. The second the prince's feet hit the stairway leading to the tarmac, the concourse buzzed back to life behind them. Travelers asked each other if the man they'd seen really was the world-famous prince, and if they knew who the woman was that he'd met.

Pia held on to the railing as she descended the stairs into the sunlight, forcing herself not to listen to the knot of gawkers forming near the windows. They'd be disappointed if they knew the truth.

"Ms. Renati?"

Pia glanced up at Federico as the driver opened the rear door for her, then realized that the prince was offering his hand to help her into the limousine.

"Oh. Thank you." Did she stick out like a goose among swans, or what?

She slipped her hand into his, and wasn't surprised to find his grasp solid, practiced. He must hand women into fancy cars every day. She ducked her head, praying she wouldn't smack it against the car roof, and

hoped that he couldn't tell how nervous his presence—
let alone his touch—made her.

Once they were buckled into the limousine's baby-
soft leather seats, the prince asked a few courteous
questions about when she'd last visited San Rimini,
what she thought Jennifer and Antony might name the
baby and whether the infant would be a boy or a girl,
since Jennifer and Antony had opted not to find out. She
managed to give some polite answers, but before they'd
even exited the airport property, their conversation
drifted off. He appeared perfectly content to ride along
quietly, facing her from the bench seat opposite hers,
but as the silence stretched on, Pia's nervousness only
grew.

The drive to the royal palace would take half an hour,
carrying them along the Strada il Teatro, San Rimini's
main thoroughfare, which ran along the very northern
coast of the Adriatic Sea. After passing the refurbished
Royal Theater near the eastern end of the Strada, they'd
climb up several miles of twisting, centuries-old cobblestoned streets to the top of San Rimini's highest hill, where
the palace overlooked the bustling casinos and quaint
shops and homes of the tiny European principality.

Pia smiled to herself, happy to see that little had
changed since her last visit. She often daydreamed of
San Rimini Bay's azure waves lapping against the
shore, the lights of the seaside casinos, and the glitz of
the country's world-class hotels. Her mouth would
water at the mere thought of the decadent desserts and
rich pasta and seafood dishes that made San Rimini fa-

mous. When working in the dusty refugee camps of the war-torn Balkans or the medical tents in disease-ravaged Africa lost its appeal, those daydreams about San Rimini put her soul at rest. Though she hadn't lived here since she was nineteen when she had left to attend college in the United States, it was home, and she relished each moment of her too-infrequent visits.

Or, she would if she wasn't sitting face-to-face with Prince Perfect and wondering about his silence. Suddenly, the half-hour drive seemed like it would take an eternity.

But hadn't he said he wanted to practice his English? Perhaps her one-syllable answers to his questions had turned him off, and he was too practiced at diplomacy to let it show.

Screwing up her courage, she tried to jump-start the conversation. "You know, it's hard for me to believe Antony and Jennifer are married, let alone that they're about to become parents."

The prince turned from the window as the limousine passed one of San Rimini's ultramodern casinos and audibly cleared his throat, making her wonder if she'd said the wrong thing. When he replied, his words, spoken with a thick accent and in a much-too-serious tone, gave her no reassurance. "They are quite happy, Ms. Renati."

Pia forced herself not to shrink back against the leather seat. She knew that she constantly put her foot in her mouth, but this was all in her mind. He couldn't be as distant or as threatening as she imagined. He was human, right? A crown didn't make him better than her. Besides, Jennifer had repeatedly described Prince Federico as a gentle, loving man, and the tabloids raved about how much he loved his two young sons.

While the tabloids weren't an ideal source of information, Jennifer wasn't the type to give false praise.

Perhaps, Pia reasoned, she simply misread his aloof demeanor at the wedding. Entirely possible, given that they'd been introduced late at night, after Prince Federico had spent the entire day assisting his brother with various prewedding events. And perhaps the loss of his wife just over a year ago had changed him, made him suspicious of unmarried women—most of whom were probably trying to coax him into a romantic relationship.

If she'd married some beautiful, perfect spouse and then lost him to an aneurysm at an early age, suddenly finding herself a young, single parent and the target of fortune hunters, she'd be a little reserved, too.

"Oh, I don't doubt they're happy, Your Highness." She shoved a blond curl away from her face, thankful that the humidity from the Adriatic couldn't make her hair look any worse than it already did after her long flight from Washington, D.C., and doubly thankful that she'd remembered to add the *Your Highness* when she spoke to him this time. "I…I just meant that it's hard for me to believe that Jennifer is about to become somebody's mother. You have to understand, during the two years I worked for Jennifer at the Haffali refugee camp, I watched her dig latrines, scrub mess tent floors and climb hills in work boots carrying jugs of water on her back. She's tough, and she cares about the people in her life. I'm sure you've been able to spend enough time around her to see that. But that doesn't exactly make her an expert on stuffed bunnies and tricycles. That's all I meant."

Federico smoothed the front of his suit jacket and nodded. "I see. Then I am glad Jennifer has found someone with maternal instincts to remain with her these next weeks before the baby's birth. I did not want her to be alone."

His expression was unreadable, his words lacking any hint of sarcasm. His sense of decorum wouldn't allow it. But if he only knew how *un*-maternal she was, he'd snatch the words back. After the lousy job her own mother had done raising her—or, more accurately, not raising her—the last thing Pia wanted was to be anyone's mother. Jennifer would be a hundred times better at mothering than Pia.

"The palace has a huge staff. And you're there, so she's not really alone." To the best of her knowledge, Federico hadn't been traveling as much as his siblings, choosing to keep close to the palace for his sons' sakes. "I think *you'd* be a good example for her."

"I believe Princess Jennifer would prefer the company of a woman. Someone who—" he shifted in the seat, as if uneasy discussing the topic of parenthood "—who knows how to keep her spirit above it. Is this the phrase in English?"

"Very close. I think you mean 'keep her spirits up.'"

"Ah, yes. That is it. She might also wish for a friend to stay with her at the hospital, should her labor begin before Antony returns."

Pia tried to ignore what he had said about the hospital. And the fact that his knee now brushed against hers, setting her hormones into overdrive. Struggling to stay focused, she continued, "I'm surprised you didn't urge your brother to stay home with her."

A vertical crease appeared in the gap between his jet-black eyebrows. "As I am sure the princess has told you, sometimes sacrifices are necessary to those in positions of power. We have duties to our subjects. Those must come before any personal desires. Anyone who spends time in the royal household learns they must also follow that duty. And above all they must keep any—" he seemed to struggle for the correct word "—private matters of the palace confidential."

Ah. So that was the prince's real concern. Jennifer had stressed during the phone call that her bed rest was being kept out of the papers. Prince Antony was in Israel, one of three nonpartisan mediators trying to hammer out a new Mideast peace agreement, and Jennifer didn't want the public to think less of him because he wasn't home with her—or for the delegates to worry that Antony might leave mid-discussion. As much as the crown prince wanted to be by his wife's side during the final six weeks of her pregnancy, Jennifer and Antony knew the fate of millions of people could depend on his calming presence at the talks.

And Federico obviously worried Pia would be less than discreet.

She fought down her chagrin. She, of all people, understood the need to save lives, which the peace talks would hopefully accomplish. More than enough of her own life had been spent cleaning up the physical carnage of political clashes. Then again, she'd never held the opinion that one could raise children and save the world at the same time. Though she'd kept her concerns from Jennifer, Pia wondered how the couple would manage both their public role as royals and their private role as parents.

The limo rolled to a stop outside the palace gates, moving ahead again after the guards ascertained the identities of the occupants. Pia leaned forward as much as her seat belt would allow, taking in the view of the royal rose gardens and the stunning facade of the palace beyond. Through the open sunroof, she could hear children laughing somewhere nearby, enjoying the late summer weather and the warm breeze blowing off the Adriatic, and wondered if it was Federico's two sons.

She eased back in her seat, resisting the urge to peek out the window to identify the source of the sound. "Your Highness, I understand the need for discretion. You shouldn't be concerned about that. But tell me— if you were in Antony's position, would you stay and negotiate, or come home to be with your family?"

Federico glanced out the window, as if he, too, wondered at the sound of the children's laughter. "I am not in Antony's position. He is the crown prince and will someday lead this country. His obligations are different than my own."

"But if you were?"

"I would do as Antony is doing. It is necessary for the good of all." Federico straightened in the seat, moving his knee away from hers.

"Ms. Renati," he continued, "right now, the delegates on both sides of the table respect my brother and the work he has accomplished on their behalf. That is an uncommon thing, and could move the process along to the benefit of all the parties involved, including San Rimini. Jennifer understands that. And so will Antony's child, someday."

He spoke with such conviction, Pia found herself agreeing with him—for the most part. She couldn't help but admire his defense of his elder brother. Federico's elegant demeanor and soft eyes mesmerized her, and whenever he spoke, the faintest smile touched his lips, as though he thought he could convince her of his arguments with nothing more than a gaze.

Given the contrast of his phenomenal baby blues against his olive skin, it probably worked nine times out of ten.

Still…

"I understand the ramifications of the peace process, Your Highness, and I admire Princess Jennifer's dedication to duty. And, of course, your willingness to support her and Antony. But don't you think that once one becomes a parent—"

The crunch of gravel beneath the limousine's wheels,

indicating that they'd arrived at the palace's rear entrance, and the approach of an older woman in a straight, woolen skirt, gave the prince the opportunity to interrupt.

"Excuse me, Ms. Renati, but this is Sophie Hunt. She is Prince Antony's private secretary and handles both Antony's and Jennifer's schedules. If you need anything during your stay at the palace, I am certain Ms. Hunt will be able to assist you."

The limousine driver stopped at the base of the palace steps where the secretary waited, then he exited and strode to the rear of the vehicle to open the door for Pia and Federico. Once again, the prince offered his hand to assist her from the car.

She shot him a smile of thanks, but reminded herself not to get used to lavish treatment. She lived in khaki pants and Birkenstocks, not Armani gowns and Jimmy Choo heels.

Introductions were made, then Federico turned his attention back to Pia and gave her a curt nod. "I leave you in good hands. And once again, I do appreciate your willingness to help, and your discretion in this matter, as does my father, King Eduardo."

So that was it. A royal reminder to keep her mouth shut and a goodbye. Pia watched him take the wide stairs into the palace by twos, all the while maintaining his upright, proper posture and athlete's grace.

Amazing.

She'd broached a topic far more personal than most would dare with a royal, yet it seemed to roll off him as if she'd mentioned nothing more contentious than the weather. Part of his upbringing, she guessed, that need to be able to hide one's emotions.

If she possessed half his sense of propriety, she wouldn't have prodded, but part of her needed to hear his response, to be assured of the fact that he cared about his children more than his job. That he did, in fact, experience emotion outside of his dedication to duty, and that the children whose laughter she'd heard on the way in to the palace grounds would continue to laugh when they saw their father, and would know that they were more than just an heir and a spare, acting as royal placeholders until Antony and Jennifer had a son.

She hoped they knew that he loved them more than anything else on earth.

"Ms. Renati, a pleasure to see you again," the secretary interrupted Pia's thoughts, her crisp, upper-class British accent sounding out of place in San Rimini. "We met briefly before Prince Antony and Princess Jennifer's wedding. You helped me direct the florists working at the cathedral, despite your own duties as a bridesmaid."

Pia tore her gaze away from Federico's retreating back and smiled at the secretary, whose friendly nature had made the woman a trusted employee of Antony and Jennifer's. "How kind of you to remember. And please, call me Pia. After riding in that limousine with His Highness, I've had enough of formality."

"I understand," she laughed. "Federico adheres to proper etiquette even more than his father." As they waited for the driver to retrieve Pia's carry-on bag from the limousine, Sophie added, "I remember all of Princess Jennifer's friends, you know. They have a tendency to marry into the diTalora family."

"So I've heard." Amanda Hutton, who'd been Jennifer's maid of honor, had stayed on after the wedding as some kind of diplomatic employee at the palace. Pia didn't know Amanda well, but read in the papers that Amanda had gone on to marry Prince Stefano, the youngest—and wildest—of the four diTalora siblings. And Princess Isabella married an American only last month.

"Well, that definitely won't happen with me," Pia promised. "I'm just here to help a pregnant friend."

But as Sophie led her through the double doors at the rear of the palace, then through one ornate mirror- and art-bedecked room after another, Pia found her thoughts returning to Prince Federico. The smooth cotton of his starched shirt, the broad expanse of his shoulders, the protective set to his mouth when he talked about Antony and Jennifer.

When they passed by a portrait of Federico laughing with his father during a national parade, Pia decided that if the prince could learn to relax a little, act a little less like he lived life by a carefully drawn script, he might be worth getting to know better. Perhaps, just perhaps, those women who mooned over the tabloid pictures of Prince Perfect were on to something.

Pia's hand instantly went to her stomach at the thought. What possessed her to think that? She wasn't that brave—she could barely keep her composure just being helped into a limousine by the man.

Okay. It had been a long, long time since she had been in a relationship. Her job didn't allow it, and her job meant everything to her. So what if Prince Federico oozed confidence and turned heads with his quiet grace? Particularly female heads. He clearly didn't approve of her, and she didn't plan to give him a second look, either. Giving a man a second look would get her exactly where Jennifer was. Pregnant. And she had no intention of ever needing one of those floral-jacketed books for herself.

Why had he given her a second look?

Federico diTalora stared out of the second floor window topping the staircase that led to the wing housing the royal family's private apartments. From his vantage point he could see Sophie standing on the outdoor steps speaking with Pia Renati while the driver fetched the blonde's well-worn carryall from the limousine's trunk.

She was a scruffy thing. Short, untamed curls everywhere. Outdoor sandals like nothing he owned. Clothes that were…what was the word? Hippie? No, she wasn't a hippie, as he understood the term. But she was close.

Earthy. Real. True to herself.

She bothered him. His initial impression of her, when she'd scurried away from him at Jennifer and Antony's wedding nearly eighteen months ago, made him wonder if the noble class unsettled her. He'd encountered that reaction more than once. The media made him, and others of the royal family, into something bigger than what they really were. Untouchable. Perfect.

How he hated that word, *perfect.* Lucrezia's death taught him he was anything but.

Given her heritage, Pia should know nobility made mistakes. She might be a commoner, but if he recalled correctly, Viscount Angelo Renati—a friend of Antony's—was her first cousin. Angelo, with his reputation for womanizing, never had to worry about the tabloids calling him "perfect." And if not through Angelo, then Pia's mother certainly could have taught Pia a thing or two about nobility, since the upper crust made up the bulk of Sabrina Renati's clientele. Which suggested that Pia's odd behavior around him meant something more.

He suspected, rather than being skittish around royalty, Pia had looked him over, judged him and seen right through his Prince Perfect exterior.

Federico adjusted the heavy, chocolate-colored curtain for a better look as Pia followed Sophie up the rear stairs and into the palace. Once the women were out of sight, he dropped the velvet panel and turned away from the window. He should be thinking about his sons, and about the problems he was having with their nanny—the third since their mother had passed away. But he found himself wanting to return to his conversation with Pia.

He knew he'd chosen duty before love when he'd married Lucrezia. They had been close friends since childhood, had understood each other, had understood the nature of royalty and the need for princes to marry well and produce heirs. They hadn't been in love, but that had never bothered them.

At least, it hadn't bothered *him* until she'd passed away, and he'd seen the difference love made in the lives of his two brothers and his sister.

Since Lucrezia's death he'd wondered if his decision to obey his duty and marry into the San Riminian aristocracy had cheated Lucrezia out of finding a loving, caring husband. When he'd voiced his concern to Stefano—the youngest of the diTalora siblings—Stef had sworn up and down that Lucrezia had entered the marriage with her eyes wide open, and that Federico shouldn't feel an ounce of guilt, that he hadn't cheated her.

Federico wasn't so sure. Lucrezia had been intelligent, beautiful and articulate. Dozens of men would have married her for love.

She had deserved better than him. He hadn't loved her enough to marry her. Romantic love wasn't the same as a love grown out of respect or familiarity.

Either way, he'd be damned if he'd cheat his children because he failed to love them with his whole heart.

Could he really be guilty of such an action? He walked down the second floor's main hallway, then turned into another, smaller hallway that led to his private apartments. Had his nannies been a disappointment because he hadn't cared enough to research them adequately? Had he failed to spend enough time with his sons to understand their needs?

He hadn't thought so. Paolo and Arturo were bright, loving children, and he adored sitting in on their music lessons or taking them on outings to local parks and museums. The mere sound of their laughter lifted his heart on the days when he wondered if there was anything to his life outside his public duties.

But Pia's words—words no one else had dared to speak to him—made him wonder.

No, he chastised himself. He was only feeling guilty because Pia Renati spoke freely, something he wasn't used to. The blonde was like no woman he'd ever met, but that didn't mean she was correct.

A squeal of pain that could only belong to Arturo, his five-year-old, stopped Federico in his tracks. He glanced out the nearest window, then heard another cry and realized that the sound had emanated from his apartments. Though Arturo constantly hurt himself, like any five-year-old, Federico jogged rather than walked along the marble-floored corridor. By the time he reached the guard seated at the entrance to his private apartments, Federico could also hear little Paolo crying and the high-pitched voice of their frustrated nanny asking them to shush.

"Your Highness." The guard stood, then slid a glance toward the door of the living quarters.

"What has happened?"

The guard held up his palms. "I do not know. But Signorina Fennini is inside."

Federico nodded, then strode through his apartments, heading for the nursery. In a serious situation, the nanny knew to summon the guard.

But when Federico pushed open the nursery door, he couldn't believe the chaos that greeted him.

Chapter Two

"Papa! Get him off me!" Arturo cried the minute he noticed Federico in the doorway.

An antique ceramic vase encircled Arturo's chubby arm, and three-year-old Paolo was attempting to pull it off, his face white with fear for his older brother. Arturo yelled again for Paolo to stop pulling, that his hand might fall off. Behind them, the nanny held the handset of the phone to her ear. From what Federico could discern, she'd called for the assistance of the palace doctor in extricating Arturo's trapped hand. At least she was doing something useful and not chatting with her friends again.

Federico went to Paolo first. The little boy's face crumpled at the sight of his father, but Federico managed to ease him away from his older brother. As Paolo let out a choked sob, the prince turned to Arturo. "Sit down and place your arm on the floor. Do not hold it in the air."

Arturo instantly quieted and plopped his bottom on the hooked car- and airplane-patterned rug covering the nursery floor, his wide eyes silently begging his father for help.

"Good." Federico sat next to Arturo, then pulled Paolo onto one knee, trying to calm the little boy while testing the vase around Arturo's arm with his fingers. It didn't seem too tight, but he didn't want to pull on it, since Paolo's attempts had only served to upset Arturo. "Can you move your fingers at all?"

Arturo sniffed and nodded. "But I can't get my hand out, Papa."

"Grandpa's doctor is on duty downstairs. He will come help you. You can be strong and wait patiently, *si?*"

The little boy squared his shoulders, and Federico ruffled his hair. "Good. You will grow to be a fine prince if you continue to be so brave."

The nanny set the phone back onto the receiver, then hurried back to the center of the room, where Federico sat with the boys. She dipped into a quick curtsey. "*Mi dispiace,* Your Highness. I called for the doctor, so he's on his way. Arturo wanted to break the vase to free his hand, but I didn't think you'd like that. It looks expensive."

"No, not if the doctor can get his hand out. Arturo could be cut by the broken pieces." Federico studied the seafoam-colored vase, recognizing it as one his late mother acquired on a trip to Turkey nearly twenty years before. It held great sentimental value, but he'd gladly sacrifice it for his son if necessary.

A moment later, the doctor arrived, and Arturo showed the older man his arm. "My soldier fell in, *Dottore*," he explained, holding up his arm and the vase with it. "I didn't mean to."

The doctor, who'd been with the family since Federico was young, gave Arturo a look of mock chastisement. "You should not go sticking your fingers in where they do not belong, Arturo. But it is not a problem. Your uncle Stefano did much worse when he was young."

Arturo's eyes widened, while Paolo started to giggle. "He did?" asked Paolo. "Uncle Stefano was *bad?*"

Seeing that the boys were in good hands, Federico set Paolo down, then stepped back to allow the doctor to inspect his patient. He met the nanny's gaze and raised an eyebrow, indicating that she should follow him to the corner of the room.

"What happened, Mona?" he asked once out of the children's hearing.

The nanny had the good sense to look apologetic. "We were taking a walk through the gardens, Your Highness, when Arturo realized he'd lost his soldier. We headed back to the nursery to search for it, and before I realized what had happened, he'd stopped and put his hand into the vase. He said he'd dropped his soldier in there."

"Why was he anywhere near that vase? It belongs on

a display pedestal near the entrance to my father's apartments. That is not the way to the gardens."

A red flush spread across the young woman's cheeks, and she began to fiddle with the hem of her gray T-shirt, which was short enough to reveal several inches of skin above her fitted black pants. Not for the first time, he wondered at the so-called "exclusive" nanny service that had referred her. He'd been told that their training program included discussions on how to dress appropriately for outdoor play while still appearing neat and polished enough to fit into a formal household. Even after spending three months with his family, Mona didn't seem to comprehend the notion that her professional appearance mattered.

Casual clothes were fine. Belly-baring, tight outfits were not.

She finally dropped the hem. "I do not know, Your Highness."

"You do not know how he came to be near King Eduardo's apartments? Or you do not know where he found the vase?" He tried to keep his voice from sounding harsh. He hated to hurt the young woman's feelings, but he wondered how closely she'd been watching Arturo. It wasn't the first time Mona lost track of him, and it simply wasn't safe for the young prince to wander the palace corridors alone. It would be too easy for him to inadvertently wander into his father's offices, interrupting an important government meeting, or to leave the secured areas and lock himself outdoors.

Or even worse, to bump into one of the large tour

groups allowed into the public rooms on the palace's first floor. Anything could happen to him then—he could be photographed, asked personal questions about his family, grabbed, or worse.

Much, much worse.

Federico tried not to think of the possibilities.

"Neither, Your Highness," Mona replied, nervousness filling her voice. "I was carrying Paolo, since he was tired from walking outside. Arturo was following right behind me, but when I turned around to ask him a question, he was gone. I thought he must have gotten distracted and taken a different route to the nursery, but when I arrived at your apartments, the guard said he hadn't seen him."

A wave of concern gripped Federico's gut. "And you did not alert the staff? Or call me? I gave you the number of the cellular phone in my limousine."

"Not long after I spoke with the guard, Arturo came around the corner, and he had the vase stuck on his hand." Her entire face had gone crimson now, and her eyes filled with tears. "I apologize. I know I should have called. I promise, it won't happen again."

Federico bit back his anger, trying to keep in mind that the nanny was new to the palace, and only nineteen herself. "All right, Mona. But please, in the future, be sure to keep the boys in your sight at all times. You are their primary protector when I'm away, and not everyone has pure motives where my children are concerned. If this happens again, we shall reconsider your employment here."

Mona nodded. "Yes, Your Highness."

"Thank you." His tone softened, and he added, "I do appreciate that you are trying. If I can do anything to make your job easier, let me know."

She replied that she would, and at that moment, a yell erupted from both boys. The doctor held up the vase. "You see, Arturo? You needed to let go of the soldier if you wished your hand to be free."

Federico ran a hand over his face, a combination of relief and exasperation running through him. Arturo had been holding on to the soldier? How could the nanny not have realized it?

How could *he* not have realized it? What kind of father was he?

Arturo rubbed his hand, slowly massaging the reddened skin back to a healthy color, then looked up at the doctor. "How do I get my soldier back? I can't leave him in there!"

The doctor laughed, then turned the vase upside down and shook it a few times, dumping the soldier into Arturo's upturned palm. "Like this. Now both of you boys be more careful, all right?"

They nodded, anxious to behave in front of their father, if not around the nanny. "Yes, *Dottore*."

The doctor took a final look at Arturo's hand to ensure the boy hadn't suffered any injury, then smiled at Federico and took his leave.

Federico crouched down in front of the boys. He might have bungled the task of freeing Arturo's hand, but he wasn't going to let the more serious aspect of the vase incident go without note. "Paolo, Arturo. What were my instructions to you?"

"Listen to Signorina Fennini," they said in unison.

"And?"

"Do. Not. Leave. Her. Sight."

"Correct." Federico focused on Arturo. "You disobeyed, yes?"

"Yes, Papa." The little boy raised his deep brown eyes to meet Federico's and tightened his fist around his soldier, as if afraid his father would take it away. "I promise not to do it again. Promise!"

"Then I shall take you at your word." He gave hugs to both boys, then turned to Mona. "I have a fundraising dinner to attend tonight for the University of San Rimini. If you need anything, I shall have my cellular phone with me."

"I'll make sure Arturo is good," Paolo assured him.

"You are only responsible for yourself, Paolo. Your brother will be good on his own. He has promised."

Federico made his way out of the nursery, stopping briefly to straighten a stack of the boys' books, then turned at the door to give his sons one last wave. Arturo had his soldier balanced precariously on a lamp near the nursery's rocking chair, his father already forgotten as he pretended that the soldier was about to leap out of an aircraft. Playing along, Paolo ran to the oversize toy box to dig for something that could push the soldier off the lamp.

And the nanny was helping him.

Federico shook his head, knowing he'd likely find

the lamp broken by the end of the evening. As he closed the door behind him, all desire to attend the dinner vanished. He fervently wished he could dismiss the nanny and spend the evening with his sons himself.

Pia Renati had been one hundred percent right. He spent far more time attending to duty than to his own children.

When he entered the main hallway, Federico's secretary fell into step beside him. Without preamble, Teodora began running down the list of events he was to attend over the next few days. Federico only half-listened. He could just imagine Pia's questions if she heard Teodora's description of his upcoming meeting with the leader of the national fishermen's association. Or the speech he was expected to deliver at the opening of a new government office building.

Federico wondered if the outspoken, curly-haired blonde could propose a solution to his dilemma as easily as she'd pinpointed it.

He doubted it.

"I've been here two weeks already, and I'm still not convinced you really need me," Pia grumbled to Jennifer as she grabbed a bottle of water from a minifridge cleverly hidden in an antique armoire in the palace apartment that the princess shared with Prince Antony. "I swear, there are more people in this place than in the White House and 10 Downing Street combined."

"There are also more royals. Downside of a big family—it requires more staff, more protection, you name it." Jennifer, whose flaming red hair and soft ivory skin made her look like a beauty queen, even nine months pregnant, let out a not-so-beautiful groan and wiggled her toes.

"But no one to fluff the princess's pillow for her?" Pia teased. "Poor baby."

Jennifer eyed the pillow elevating her feet. "Ha, ha. Even with all the staff in the world, you're still the only person I can gripe to about my swollen ankles. Or about the fact I've been stuck in this room forever. With you, I'm as comfortable as when I'm alone."

"I'm not sure that's a compliment."

Pia screwed the top off the water bottle, then looked up to see Jennifer giving her a pointed glance. "It *is* a compliment. I don't feel like my privacy's being invaded with you here—I'm just hanging out with a friend. And the best part is that you don't slink around the room as if you think I'm some icon you can't speak to or look at directly. I'll tell you, this life has taken me a lot of getting used to."

Jennifer reached forward on the bed to rearrange the pillow, but gave up when Pia handed her the bottle of water.

"It's nothing like Haffali, is it, Jen?" Pia asked as she took over adjusting Jennifer's pillow so that her feet stayed elevated. "I mean, your nails are done, your hair looks perfect, and swollen ankles or not, you look like a real princess. No one would ever guess you once ran a refugee camp in the middle of a war zone."

Jennifer let out a halfhearted laugh. "No, I guess

not. I don't miss the war zone part of it, but I do miss helping people. Stuck in bed like this, I'm even missing the charity events. I feel completely useless."

"I think," Pia angled a look at Jennifer's expanding midsection, "you should focus on yourself and your baby right now. Don't get me wrong—we missed your help at camp when you ran off and married a prince, of all people." She waved a hand at their posh surroundings for emphasis. "But the money you and Antony raised, and the students you sponsored to come work at the camp through your scholarship program, helped us relocate the refugees and close the camp months earlier than we could have otherwise. And then you went out of your way to recommend me to World AIDS Relief, to make sure I could find another job. You deserve a break after all your work. Enjoy it."

When Jennifer didn't respond, Pia added, "If you absolutely have to do something, brainstorm a way to expand your scholarship program. You can do that just as well in a royal bedchamber as you did while working in a rusty trailer in the Balkans. Better, even."

"Goody, goody," Jennifer took a long sip of water, then twirled her finger in the air as if to say, *whoopee.* "Glad to know I can be mistaken for a beached whale and be useful at the same time."

A knock at the door interrupted them and Pia excused herself to answer it. She greeted the guard, then returned to Jennifer carrying an armload of mail, including at least two dozen handwritten letters and three boxes. "I don't know how you find time for all this,"

Pia commented as she dumped everything on the bed next to Jennifer.

"I usually don't," Jennifer admitted, turning over an envelope to read the engraved return address on the flap. "Sophie handles most of the invitations and routine correspondence. But I'm sick of sitting here and asked her if I could do it to break up my routine."

Pia grunted in agreement as she retrieved a sterling silver letter-opener from Jennifer's corner desk, a gift the princess had received from Antony shortly after their marriage.

"Looks like I can actually put you to work today." Jennifer peered in at the contents of one of the boxes. "I ordered this camera for Antony's birthday, but they forgot the gift wrap."

She lifted the camera case out of the shipping box to show Pia. "I wanted to give it to him this weekend, since he'll be able to come home for a day before the peace talks resume. But there's no way I can go all the way to the gift-wrapping room to do it myself. And if I give it to one of the staff, I know they'll spill the beans—"

"This place has a gift-wrapping *room?*" Pia set the letter opener on top of the pile of invitations and letters on the bed. "You must be kidding."

Jennifer handed Pia the camera case and shrugged. "I know. Outrageous, isn't it? You don't mind doing the wrapping, though, I hope?"

"'Course not. That's what I'm here for," Pia replied as she turned the camera over in her hands. Antony would be thrilled with the gift, since he'd be able to use it to shoot photos of his new baby. "I need something to do besides sitting here handing you tissue or getting you water. I don't think I've ever been this lazy in my life."

"Me, either," Jennifer admitted. "I just keep telling myself it's good for the baby, and that it can't last much longer. Thirty-six weeks down, four to go." She gave Pia directions to the gift-wrapping room, which was located behind the palace's main kitchen, then waved her off.

Pia strode out of Jennifer and Antony's ornate private apartments with the camera tucked under her arm, then made her way toward the wide marble staircase leading down to the kitchen. Fresh air from the palace gardens blew in through the open windows lining the hallway, and her steps grew lighter as she breathed in the smell of the freshly cut lawn. Even though wrapping a gift would normally strike her as a mundane task, today it felt liberating.

As much as Pia loved Jennifer, it had been tough spending much of the two weeks since arriving at the palace sitting still, either reading books in Jennifer's room while the princess napped, or bringing Jennifer whatever she needed so she was on her feet as little as possible. Jennifer seemed healthy enough, and claimed to feel good, but the unexplained bleeding she'd experienced a few weeks before had worried the obstetrician enough to urge her not to take any chances. Antony had agreed with the doctor's assessment, despite knowing his bride would be unable to accompany him on local outings, let alone on his trip to the Middle East.

As slothful as Pia felt most days, she knew her presence made Jennifer less lonely, now that Antony was in Israel and difficult to reach. It also reassured Antony to know that someone was watching out for his wife.

And, as Jennifer said, it gave the princess an outlet for griping about her pregnancy discomforts without fear it would end up as a topic of conversation among the palace staff. Or worse, fodder for the tabloids, should they hear of it.

Like Jennifer, Pia was used to moving around, keeping her body as fit as her mind. Reading a book a day—or more—and watching endless hours of television quickly lost its allure. Instead, over the last few days Pia found her mind wandering to her job. Once Antony returned home and Jennifer had safely delivered her baby, Pia could move on to her next assignment for World AIDS Relief, the Washington, D.C.-based nonprofit group for which she worked. This time she'd be headed for sub-Saharan Africa, where she'd be in charge of the final construction details and staffing of three residences for children who'd lost their parents in Africa's exploding AIDS epidemic. Though the three facilities wouldn't be nearly enough to handle the demand, she took comfort in the thought that at least some orphaned children might find a place to live, fresh food and a chance at a basic education. Not to mention the love and comfort the relief workers offered in abundance.

While the centers were under construction, Pia would have the opportunity to travel through Mozambique, South Africa and Zimbabwe, educating young women about the realities of HIV. Hopefully she could prevent them from contracting the terrible virus and leaving behind even more orphans. Though the accommodations wouldn't be nearly as comfortable as what she had now—nothing on earth was as lavish as the San Rimini Royal Palace—she relished the chance to help people who needed her. To see the difference she made in the life of a poor, needy child or a desperate young woman.

As Pia made her way down the red-carpeted marble staircase, she reminded herself that her time with Jennifer was a vacation, and that she should try harder to enjoy it. Within a few short weeks she'd probably miss the chance to put her feet up and chat with Jennifer about ordinary things.

She reached the bottom of the wide stairs and took the hallway to her left. Unable to resist her curiosity, she took a quick peek inside the king's small private study, where Jennifer said he kept his personal collection of books and family photographs and could often be found reading late at night, winding down after a busy day.

Four rooms beyond the library, Pia pushed through the heavy oak doors leading to the diTalora family's private dining room, which they used for casual breakfasts and lunches, as opposed to the ultra-formal state dining room located at the other end of the palace, where visiting dignitaries could come and go through the front gates.

Though the bells of San Rimini's largest cathedral, the nearby Duomo, tolled the noon hour loudly enough to be heard inside the palace, the dining room was unoccupied. Princess Isabella and her new husband, Nick, had just finished their honeymoon, but had stopped in New York on their way home to attend the opening of an exhibit of San Riminian art. Prince Stefano and his wife of nearly a year—Jennifer's friend Amanda—were in England on a long-overdue state visit. And King Eduardo rarely enjoyed a meal that wasn't part of one meeting or another.

Pia hadn't expected Federico to be here eating lunch. Really, she hadn't. Still, she was surprised to find herself disappointed at his absence.

She hadn't seen the prince since their brief limousine ride, but found that she couldn't get him off her mind, much as she tried to distract herself with reading material or thoughts about her new assignment in Africa. Pia guessed that with the rest of the family gone and Jennifer eating her meals in her own room, Federico and his sons ate in his private apartments.

She lingered for a moment to study the dining room's oak-paneled walls, which were filled with antique tapestries, and its long, heavy table. For most people, such a room would be considered ostentatious. But for the diTalora family, an oak table near the palace kitchen—whatever the decor of the room—constituted casual dining. They might even show up in polo shirts and slacks here, as opposed to their usual business- or formal-wear.

The refugees she'd worked with would be stunned

to enter such a room, let alone dine in it. And Pia herself felt the same way as she strode the palace halls or peeked into its sumptuously decorated rooms. It had taken her several days to accustom herself to the beauty of the private palace apartment Jennifer and Antony shared, though Jennifer claimed to have toned it down since marrying Antony and moving in.

Unbidden, an image of what Federico's apartments must look like leaped into her mind. They would be formal, of course. More so than Antony and Jennifer's, given his stiff personality—and his late wife's. Rich fabrics. Children's toys arranged in perfect order. Pricey gifts from foreign dignitaries on every shelf and tabletop. A huge bed with expensive silk sheets—

Pia shook off that image, wondering if Federico had as difficult a time adjusting to spending time in the palace as she had. Though Federico grew up in the royal residence surrounded by luxury, before Lucrezia's death he'd spent most of his time traveling, representing San Rimini abroad. His life had been filled with adventure—meeting dignitaries, hammering out political and economic agreements, attending endless parties and charity events. He'd probably seen it all, from countries struggling for survival to superpowers with more economic clout than some continents. He'd visited downtrodden hospital patients without two pennies to rub together, met destitute children without parents, and then gone to visit the well-heeled political leaders who sat behind expensive antique desks only miles away. As prince, it all came with the job description.

But now that he was the sole parent to Arturo and Paolo, Federico had severely curtailed his public duties. It couldn't have been easy for him, spending all his time in one place, just as it hadn't been easy for her over the past two weeks.

But her stay was only temporary. Federico had a permanent adjustment to make.

"Don't think about him," she cautioned herself aloud as she crossed the empty room, her footsteps echoing across the hardwood. She strode through the doors to the tiled palace kitchen, but the image of Federico's high cheekbones and wide, intelligent blue eyes refused to leave her mind.

How could one man, someone she'd only spent half an hour or so talking to, occupy her thoughts to the exclusion of all else?

Boredom. Had to be. Once she was back at work, she'd forget her encounter with Prince Perfect.

After entering the kitchen, one of the cooks steered her toward the door of the palace's old wine cellar, which had apparently been converted into a gift-wrapping center when renovations were made to the kitchen and a new wine cellar constructed. The room still felt like a wine cellar, however, with its Italian tile floors, windowless walls and cool temperature.

A large metal table, with enough space to wrap multiple gifts at once, dominated the room. Along the far wall ribbons of various colors hung on oversize spools. To her left and right, where fine wines had once been displayed, wrapping paper appropriate for every occasion imaginable now filled racks from floor to ceiling. On either side of the door were clear plastic chests of tape, bows and gift bags. A paper cutter and several pairs of scissors rested on top of each chest. In a separate organizer, elegant white cards and their accompanying envelopes bore the diTalora family crest, identifying all gifts as coming from the royal family. A number of fountain pens stood in an expensive-looking pen cup nearby.

It put most department store gift-wrapping areas to shame.

Pia set the camera and film on the metal table, then perused the wrapping paper, finally settling on a blue and silver plaid. Festive, yet gentlemanly. She pulled the roll from the wall, placed it on the table, then studied the oversize paper cutter, trying to ascertain the proper way to position the paper in the contraption. Once she had figured it out, she loaded the paper onto the spool.

"I believe you have it backward, Ms. Renati."

Pia jumped, nearly slicing her hand under the blade of the cutter. "Um, Your Highness. I didn't hear you come in."

Federico smiled from the doorway—a polite but reserved smile—then strode to her side, removed the paper from the spool and repositioned it. "If you place it this way, you will get a cleaner cut." He frowned, then cocked his head. "Is it correct English to say a 'cleaner' cut?" He repeated the phrase in Italian, to make sure Pia understood his meaning.

"That's correct, Your Highness."

He nodded, as if pleased that he'd come up with the proper phrase, then turned his attention back to the paper cutter. He was about to trim the paper for her, but glanced at the design and stopped short. "Is this for Princess Jennifer?"

"It's a gift for Antony. From the princess."

"Then you have made a good selection."

He cut the paper to the appropriate size, then slid the sheet across the table to where she had the camera.

"I don't mean to be nosy, Your Highness—"

"Please, Ms. Renati. You are a guest of our household and will likely be here for several more weeks. You may feel free to call me Federico."

"Okay. Federico." Somehow, it didn't seem appropriate. Not when he still spoke so formally, using phrases like "you may feel free" as if he were granting royal permission, while she had a vocabulary peppered with Americanisms. But she wasn't going to go against his wishes.

Besides, she liked the way his name rolled off her tongue. "Federico" sounded strong, masculine. Ideal for the powerful man standing before her.

"I was wondering what you were doing here," she continued. "I can't imagine you often wander around this part of the palace."

He smiled at that. This time, it was a genuine, I'm-finding-you-entertaining grin that warmed her inside. "No, I do not. But I have a gift for Princess Jennifer." He gestured to the end of the table, and Pia realized he'd set down a book as he'd entered the room. She read the title aloud, unable to keep the surprise out of her voice. *"The Ultra-Hip Mom's Guide To Baby's First Year?"*

"I purchased it on a trip to the United States a few years ago. I thought Princess Jennifer might appreciate it."

Pia slid him a sideways glance. "Hate to accuse you of lying, but Jennifer wasn't pregnant a few years ago."

"No." He hesitated. "So I will tell you a secret."

Pia raised an eyebrow.

"I purchased it for Lucrezia, when she was pregnant with Arturo. But she never found the time to read it. I tried to find a new copy for Jennifer, since I thought it might be to her liking, but it was not available in San Rimini, so…" He held up his palms in a gesture of surrender. "I am afraid you have found me out."

Pia gave the book a pointed look, then grinned at the prince. "In America, that's what's referred to as 're-gifting.' People sometimes do it when they receive a gift they don't care for, but can't return."

A stunned look passed over Federico's face. "Re-gifting? And this is common?"

Pia tried—without success—not to crack up at the prince's obvious shock. "Scandalous, isn't it? But don't worry about it. Jennifer's the one who told me about re-gifting in the first place. She'll be touched by the present, re-gifted or not."

"So you will keep my secret?"

Pia drew a finger across her chest diagonally each way. "Of course."

"Thank you." He turned, surveying the numerous

rolls of paper. While he did so, Pia discreetly looked from Federico back to the book again. No, she couldn't imagine Lucrezia cracking that spine. But Federico, buying a book on how to be a hip mom? It was equally hard to picture. And he'd tried to buy it twice! She began to suspect there was more to the prince than simply good looks and an aristocratic title.

"Ms. Renati?"

She tore her gaze from the book to find the prince studying her. "Pia. Please."

His eyes warmed. "Pia, then. Would you be so kind as to help me select a paper for Princess Jennifer's gift? While I am familiar with my brother's taste, I do not know hers as well as I should."

Pia's nerves settled. "I'd love to." She studied the rolls, finally selecting a simple tone-on-tone beige paper with a scroll and leaf design.

"Should I not use a paper like this?" He fingered a roll with pink lambs and yellow rabbits on a powder blue background.

Pia pulled a face. "Save that for when the baby arrives. This gift is for Jennifer. You want something elegant. Pretty."

Federico shrugged and looked back at the beige paper. "It is fortunate you were here. I would have made a fool of myself."

Pia put her hand on his arm and squeezed. "No. Most men in your position wouldn't have taken the time to buy such a thoughtful gift, let alone wrap it themselves. I think it's sweet."

Chapter Three

Realizing what she'd done, Pia yanked her hand away from Federico's arm. She stepped forward so she couldn't meet his gaze, then took the roll of beige paper off the wall and handed it to the prince.

Working side by side, she and Federico wrapped their gifts. Except for the rustle of gift wrap being cut and folded, or the occasional sound of tape being torn from its dispenser, the room was silent.

What possessed her to touch his arm like that? Even through the sleeve of his starched, blue button-down shirt, during that brief touch, she'd become aware of the corded strength of his arm and the heat of his body. She'd done it to offer comfort, as she would to any of the hundreds of refugees she'd helped over the years. But this was the first time she'd experienced a physical reaction to such a simple touch, and the thought of it unsettled her.

"It is finished." Federico held up his package. "Would a white bow be appropriate?"

Pia nodded, and Federico turned to select one from the chests near the door while she folded the paper around the end of the camera box. As she taped down the final flap, something brushed against her elbow. She glanced down to see that Federico had sent a large blue bow sliding across the metal table to her.

"I believe Antony would like that one."

She let out a breath, realizing as she did so how nervous his silence made her. "Thank you. It matches perfectly."

She ripped another piece of tape off the dispenser and attached the bow to the box. "See, you do know what you're doing. You didn't need me."

"I beg to differ."

She looked up to retort, but in that moment, she caught a flicker in his eyes that made her wonder if he was flirting. But then he pushed open the door to the kitchen, and the sound of morning banter between the palace cook and the dishwashers broke the spell.

"Shall we take the gifts to Princess Jennifer?" Federico braced the door open with his arm, indicating that he expected her to lead the way.

"Ah, sure." She grabbed the camera and ducked past him. They crossed through the kitchen and dining room, and as they walked the way back to Jennifer's apartments, he described each of the rooms they passed, their history, and what artifacts they possessed. All the while, Pia tried not to think of how handsome he looked in his shirtsleeves, how clean and wonderful he smelled as he walked beside her, or how his gracious manners and the rich cadence of his voice as he described his home made her feel as spoiled as if she'd been born with a crown herself.

Widower with two kids, she reminded herself. *All wrong, even if he is a gentleman.*

As if summoned by her thoughts, the thumping of small feet and the sound of children's unrestrained laughter echoed from the second floor. Federico frowned to himself, and Pia got the sense that his sons weren't permitted to play in the hallway.

Federico didn't alter his pace, however. Instead, he merely commented, "Those are my sons, Arturo and Paolo. I suspect you will have the opportunity to meet them before they return to the nursery."

"Sounds like they're having a fun morning."

"Yes." His voice was calm, even. But given the grave look on the prince's face, Pia decided it wouldn't be at all fun to be in the nanny's shoes when Federico reached the top of the stairs.

Just as Pia reached the top step and sought out the source of the laughter, something small and brown flashed in her peripheral vision. Immediately, a bolt of pain sliced her temple, nearly knocking her to the ground. As a reflex, she put a hand to her forehead, her fingertips meeting torn skin. She registered a sharp intake of breath coming from across the hall at the same time the rapid pound-pound-pound of children's feet abruptly stopped.

A hand-carved boomerang lay at her feet. Federico bent to retrieve it, then met her surprised gaze.

"Pia, you are injured!" He withdrew a crisp white handkerchief from his pocket, pressed it to her temple, then herded her toward an antique-looking upholstered chair under one of the hallway's broad windows.

"It's all right," Pia mumbled. She'd suffered enough scrapes and tumbles in her line of work to know that no permanent damage was done. No feeling faint, no dizziness. But as she reached up to take the handkerchief from Federico and hold it to her head, her hand brushed against his, and she realized that her blood soaked both the cloth and his fingers.

The panicked cry of a child suddenly registered in her mind, and Pia turned to see two young boys cowering against a doorjamb. Though they both had expressive brown eyes very different from Federico's blue ones, their skin tone, facial features and dark hair were identical to the prince's, leaving no doubt as to their heritage.

The younger boy's face fell as she met his gaze, his eyes squinching shut against his tears, and his mouth dropped open with the heartbroken sadness of a child who realizes that he's unintentionally injured another. The older boy stood behind him, clearly more concerned about his father's reaction than his brother's tears.

However, when Pia caught his eye, he stepped forward. He shrugged and mumbled, "*Mi dispiace,* signorina. I hope it doesn't hurt too much." Then he looked to Federico. "I didn't mean to, Papa."

Federico pinned his older son with a look that spoke volumes as to his displeasure. "Arturo, where is Signorina Fennini?"

"I am here, Your Highness." The nanny ran up behind Arturo and Paolo, her breathing ragged, her expression twice as distressed as that of the small boys. "I am terribly sorry, but—"

"Please call my driver, Signorina Fennini. I must take Ms. Renati to the hospital."

Federico must have sensed the protest on Pia's lips, because he turned to her and explained, "We have a palace doctor for emergencies, but I believe you will need stitches. It should be done in a hospital, so we can lessen the chance you will be marked…" He frowned, then added, "You understand. *Cicatrice?*"

A scar? Not from a little cut to her forehead. "I don't think you need to—"

"I shall call right now," the nanny interrupted, then turned in the opposite direction.

"Signorina Fennini?"

The nanny turned to face Federico, and Pia's heart sank at his tone. "After you have spoken with my driver, please call my secretary. Explain what happened, and ask her to arrange for someone else to watch the children tonight."

From the embarrassed look on the nanny's face and

the determined one on Federico's, Pia realized she'd just witnessed the nanny being fired. She said nothing, though she felt a wave of sympathy for the young woman.

And then, an overwhelming feeling of déjà vu. How old had she been on her own first babysitting job? Not much younger than the nanny. It also ended badly, leaving her with hurts greater than any she had suffered from the boomerang.

Once the nanny left, Pia forced herself to ignore her throbbing head and winked at the boys. "Accidents happen, guys. It's okay." She hoped that Federico got the message, as well. Hopefully, he'd give the young girl a second chance.

Both boys still looked upset, so Pia used her free arm to make a muscle. "See? I'm tough. Getting banged in the head is no big deal."

The older boy, Arturo, looked down at his feet, but she could see he hid a smile.

"I'm Pia Renati. What's your name?" Pia asked the younger boy.

"Paolo."

"Paolo. That's one of my favorite names! My father's name was Paolo, and it's my cousin Angelo's middle name."

Arturo raised his head, his face alight. "Viscount Renati? He's a friend of my uncle Antony's."

"He's very nice," Paolo whispered. "He sent Aunt Jennifer pretty flowers after she told us she had a baby growing in her tummy."

Pia grinned, trying to ignore her worsening headache. "That sounds like Angelo."

Beside her, however, Federico grunted.

She didn't spend much time with Angelo, since they possessed such opposite personalities. But hearing Federico's disapproving noise, it occurred to her that the prince must be acquainted with her cousin—and Angelo's reputation for shameless flirting, especially when the press was around to see and photograph him. No wonder Federico suspected that she might not be discreet about Jennifer's condition.

Despite Angelo's public persona, Pia knew he would never give personal information about the royal family to tabloid reporters. He respected the royal family and valued his friendship with Antony too much. Maybe she could have Jennifer set Federico straight at some point. It would be one less reason for the prince to worry about her.

Which, given the concern etched on his face as he reached over to lift the handkerchief and study her forehead, was a good thing.

"It's really not that bad, Federico," she assured him as she pressed the handkerchief back to her forehead. "Head wounds tend to bleed a lot. Doesn't mean they're serious."

He shot a pointed look at the boys. "They should not have been throwing that indoors."

"You were aiming for the window, weren't you, Arturo?" Pia joked. "It *is* open. So that's almost like being outside."

Arturo put a hand over his mouth to hide his grin from his father, and Pia felt better, knowing the little boy was finally at ease. However, Paolo continued to stare at her, wide-eyed.

"Paolo, can you do me a favor? Look out the window and see if you can see your father's car coming."

Paolo moved to the window and stood on tiptoe to get his chin over the level of the sill. "Not yet." He looked over his shoulder and shot her a shy smile. "But I see grandpa."

A few seconds later, King Eduardo reached the top of the stairs. Apparently done with his duties for the day, he wore a pressed pair of beige slacks and a tailored black shirt that made him look far younger than his age, which she knew to be in the midfifties. His sharp gaze took in the boys, the boomerang, and her, sitting near the window. Having sized up the situation, he waved the boys to his side. Pia got the feeling he was used to commanding those around him.

Pia felt she should stand, but the king waved for her to keep her seat. "You are injured. Please, there is no need for formality." He shifted his focus to Federico. "You are taking her to the hospital, yes?"

"Yes."

Even if she hadn't seen his face on hundreds of newspaper stands, or on San Rimini's coins, she'd know Eduardo diTalora to be a king simply by his confident demeanor and the ease with which he directed those around him.

"I am finished with my appointments for today," the

king told his son, "so I shall watch Arturo and Paolo. I can take them to the old armory and show them the weapons and suits of armor their uncle Nick has restored. It will be entertaining, and they can learn about San Rimini's medieval history, as they should."

"Thank you, Father, that would be appreciated." Federico gestured toward a nearby chair, where he'd deposited the wrapped gifts. "Could you also see that these are delivered to Princess Jennifer, and let her know what has happened?"

"Of course."

The king had each boy pick up a gift, then he focused on Pia. "Will Princess Jennifer need assistance while you're away? I can summon someone to stay with her."

Pia shook her head, her temple pounding as she did so. "I think she'd prefer the privacy, Your Serene Highness. And I'll be back as soon as possible."

After offering an apology for his grandsons' antics, and a wish for her speedy recovery, the king ushered the boys down the stairs.

"Thank you for showing such kindness to my sons," Federico said once the king and the young princes were out of earshot. His gaze fixed on her bloodied forehead, but despite the lack of eye contact, his words carried enough emotion to let her know he was truly grateful. "You have a natural ability with children."

She waved it off. "Comes from working with so many in refugee camps, I suppose." She knew saying a few kind words to a troubled child, whether in a war-torn camp or in a royal palace, didn't translate into anything approaching "natural ability," not compared with what the full-time duty of parenting required, but she didn't care to contradict the prince. Not when he was saying such kind words to her, or holding his own handkerchief to her head.

Outside the window Pia heard the crunch of tires on the gravel drive. Federico glanced outside to ensure it was his car approaching, then leaned down, warning her to hold the handkerchief tight against her temple, then lifted her out of the chair and into his arms.

"Your Highness—"

"Federico."

"You…you really don't need to carry me. I'm entirely capable of walking. And I'm getting blood on your shirt."

He tightened his hold. "I have others. Now put your free arm around my shoulders. I do not wish to drop you on the stairs. That would certainly be worse than anything my sons have done to you today."

Pia did as he asked, and as her palm flattened against his upper back and the soft fabric of his shirt brushed her cheek, she decided what his sons had done wasn't so bad.

Federico couldn't believe the knot of press photographers gathered outside the hospital's front door.

He wondered what, exactly, the press had heard— that he'd fired his third nanny in just over one year, that a palace guest had been injured, that his children were the cause of the injury, or worst of all, that he'd been seen carrying a bleeding-but-beautiful blonde from his private car into San Rimini's largest hospital.

He groaned inwardly. Whichever it was, he'd probably shot his reputation as the grieving widower prince who never made a public misstep in one quick afternoon. Not that he would change any of his actions.

He shifted the window blinds for a better look at the photographers and their setup. When he took Pia back to the palace, they'd have to use a back exit and hope the press hadn't covered it. If the reporters believed he had a personal connection to Pia, they'd dog her for weeks in hopes of breaking a story on a royal romance. Not only would that be disturbing to Pia, but their pursuit would likely result in the press discovering Princess Jennifer's prescribed bed rest.

And that would be a *real* story. One that could affect the peace talks and millions of lives as a result.

Federico turned away from the window of the small private room where the staff had placed Pia, taking a seat in a well-worn chair to wait while the doctor finished placing a bandage over her injury. As Pia had argued, the wound wasn't nearly as bad as he'd feared, requiring only three or four stitches.

Federico's level of guilt, however, hadn't lessened. His gut constricted at the thought that he'd been responsible for Pia's injury. She'd taken it in stride, even trying to console the boys. While he appreciated how well she related to them, and how effectively she'd calmed them, he finally understood how his parents had felt when Stefano got into a wrestling match with two other boys in kindergarten and the matter became tabloid fodder.

As if he'd failed as a parent.

How could he have let his sons get out of his control? And to the extent that someone had gotten injured?

The doctor gave Pia instructions for keeping the bandaged area clean, then turned to Federico. "I believe she will heal quickly, Your Highness."

"*Grazie*. I appreciate your prompt attention. And please send the bill to the palace. I do not wish for Ms. Renati to be responsible."

Pia began to argue, but Federico raised a hand to stop her. "Please. It is the least I can do."

After the doctor nodded and took his leave, Pia shot him an exasperated look. "I am perfectly capable of handling my own medical bills. I have insurance."

"This accident was my fault. It would be dishonorable to allow you to deal with insurance. Your focus must be on your recovery."

She shook her head, making her blond curls bounce. "There's no 'recovery' to focus on. I'm not an invalid. And it's not your fault, anyway. This could have happened to anyone. Kids do these things."

"Not mine."

She hopped off the table where the doctor had been attending her. "I don't mean to offend, but they're children. Royal or not, they have accidents."

He puffed out a breath. "True. I try to be understanding, but unfortunately, they are held to a different standard than other children. The sooner they learn that, the easier it will be for them. It was the same for me, when I was a child."

Without warning, she placed her hand on the back of his, where it rested on the arm of the chair. Her soft skin warmed him, giving him comfort. But unlike the reassuring touch she'd offered in the gift-wrapping room, this time, she left her hand where it was. "It must've been difficult, growing up as you did, in the public eye."

"Perhaps." He looked down at her fingers, enjoying the touch of a woman without fear that she wanted something from him. "But I learned to behave, learned to fulfill my role in the family. I had no choice."

And it hadn't ended in childhood. It continued with his marriage to Lucrezia, and in the way he raised his children now. It affected the way he related to anyone and everyone whose life crossed paths with his.

He forced himself to project calm, despite the feel of Pia's fingertips softly caressing his knuckles, drawing away his frustration. He could grow used to her soft touch—had even enjoyed carrying her into his waiting car and then into the hospital. Too much, he feared.

How long had it been since he'd shared himself with a woman? Since Lucrezia's death, at least. And even then, Lucrezia had been the choice of his parents, not someone who'd come into his life by chance, offering friendship and support, yet asking nothing in return.

Unfortunately, Pia's pure-hearted gesture made him all the more susceptible to her other charms—her clean, freckle-faced blond beauty, her unassuming attitude, her warm, female touch. For a brief moment, he wondered what she'd do if he pulled her down and gave her a kiss. Would she brush him aside? Panic?

Or return it?

He swallowed hard. He couldn't think about Pia Renati, not in that way. No matter how much he enjoyed talking with her, no matter how wonderfully she treated his sons or how attractive he found her, he simply couldn't handle the public response to his having a romantic life. *Any* romantic life. Nor could he handle it personally—he'd confused friendship and comfort with love once before, and swore never to do it again.

She hesitated for a moment, as if sensing the turmoil within him. She withdrew her hand, slowly, but maintained eye contact. "I hope you'll forgive me for butting in, but you didn't need to be angry with the nanny. I would hate to see her fired because I didn't duck in time."

A nurse walked by, slowing her pace to peek in the door as she passed. Realizing their private room probably wasn't so private, Federico stood and gestured for Pia to lead the way into the hall. "We should go. I think they need the bed for other patients."

Once they were in the empty mint-green hall leading out of the emergency wing, he picked up their earlier conversation. "Do not concern yourself over the nanny. First, you cannot be expected to dodge boomerangs in the royal palace. Second, this was, unfortunately, not the first incident. So please, do not feel that the nanny's problems are any of your doing. They are not."

He wanted to say more, but they had arrived at the nurses' station, where Federico had promised the doctor he'd stop to speak with the staff and shake hands. For the first time he could recall, he had no wish to socialize with his family's subjects, an act that had become second nature to him.

He wanted to talk to Pia. Wanted to convince her he hadn't mistreated the nanny, and that he tried to be tolerant of his children and their rambunctious play. Hadn't he given the nanny every opportunity? And couldn't Pia see how much he loved his sons? Didn't she know he'd lay down his life for them?

Still, her simple questions challenged him to try harder.

Within a few minutes, his driver approached the nurses' station, giving him the opportunity to take his leave and to give Pia the chance to return to the palace and rest.

"I fear we will not make as quiet an exit as we did an entrance," Federico's driver, a sixtyish man who'd been with the family since Federico was a boy, commented as he led them down an isolated staff-only hallway to avoid curious stares. "There are reporters at every door."

"Why don't you bring the car to the west entrance," Federico suggested. "If we cannot escape them by leaving through the rear, we may as well face them and answer their questions. But I would like you nearby, with the car running, so we can leave as soon as possible."

The driver gave a businesslike nod, then walked ahead of them to retrieve the car.

"I don't need to talk to reporters, do I?" Worry lines furrowed Pia's brow. "I'm not good at that sort of thing. I wouldn't have the foggiest notion what to say. And I'm a total mess. Just look at me!"

"They will most likely focus on me. If you stand back, they should leave you alone." He smiled. "But if not, do not worry. You look fine, especially considering the afternoon you have had."

"I wish I had a mirror." A nervous edge crept into her voice as she added, "I'm sure my mascara has smeared, and—"

"Stop." He reached out and spun her to face him in the empty hall. The fluorescent hospital lights cast her skin in a less-than-flattering shade of yellow, but that wouldn't affect her outside. And he wasn't sure how her hair was supposed to look, but the tangle of curls seemed no more out of place than usual. He pulled a stray piece of white lint from the front of her summer-weight V-necked sweater, then tucked a loose curl behind her ear. "Your mascara looks fine. Do you have any lipstick?"

"Nope. No purse, no lipstick. I look washed out, don't I?"

He gave her a smile meant to reassure. "Not at all. I simply thought it would take the attention away from the bandage on your forehead."

"Is it that bad?"

"No. In fact," he reached up to trace the outline of

the white gauze, "you look wonderful for a woman who's just had stitches." And he meant it. Most women would have fallen apart when told they'd face dozens of reporters after a day like hers. But Pia possessed an inner strength and quiet confidence he admired. He'd bet his father's crown that she'd never been one for drama. She was too sweet, too unflappable.

And quite unlike any of the over-perfumed, over-styled women who frequented palace soirees, who only spoke to him for the purpose of moving ahead socially.

"That's not saying a lot." Pia's breath caressed his face as she spoke, and he caught a whiff of the clean, fruity scent of her shampoo. "But if you think I look fine, then I'll take your word for it."

"Good."

"Besides, you have blood all over your shoulder—"

"I told you, I have other shirts. And perhaps it will not show on camera."

He bent down and dropped a soft kiss near her bandage. He intended it to be a quick peck, a confidence boost before she faced the cameras outside. But his lips lingered against her soft skin; his eyes closed as he savored the forbidden sensation of her curls brushing his face.

He heard her quick intake of breath, felt her fingertips feather against his chest. In that moment, his carefully scheduled, precisely planned world came undone.

Chapter Four

So this was what it felt like to act on lust.

A soft gasp escaped Pia's lips as their mouths met. They shared a long, tender kiss, as Federico forced himself to breathe, to hold back from the warmth and comfort and passion he knew she possessed, despite the fact that every ounce of his being wanted what she had to offer. There could be no crossing of boundaries.

But even keeping their kiss on a schoolboy level, he knew it was too late. For the first time in his life, he acted on impulse, allowing his body and his desires to rule the moment. Kissing Pia—a commoner who didn't automatically extend her hand so he could help her into his limousine, who protested when he carried her, who he suspected preferred sweatpants to skirts, and who spoke to his children as if she understood their impulses—

meant surrendering to every temptation he'd been taught to avoid since childhood. Pia was a woman impossible for someone in his station, with his duties, to even consider.

Yet here he was, in one of the few moments of his life not taking place before cameras or dignitaries—or under his father's watchful eye—and damn if he wasn't considering it.

He broke the kiss, reluctantly, unwilling to keep his lips more than a whisper away from hers. He used both hands to swipe her blond curls back from her face, and saw her eyes fill with a longing that likely mirrored his own.

As much as he wanted her, as much as his body ached to give her a full-blown, earth-shattering kiss, to see where it might lead and whether it could quench his desire, he couldn't do it.

He couldn't even handle the fact that he *wanted* to a kiss her, to taste her, to feel her body pressed to his. And he certainly couldn't handle the risk of the press seeing him as anything other than Prince Perfect, the one diTalora who lived up to their ideal of a San Riminian prince. In the long run, it would hurt Pia, his family, and his country.

Leading her on—kissing her again—would be wrong.

"Pia," the sound of his voice cut through the silence of the empty hallway. "I—"

He lost his train of thought as her fingers toyed with the top button of his shirt.

"You what?" She looked up then. Her gaze locked with his, and a connection he'd never had with another human being sizzled between them.

All thought of ideals fled his mind as he closed his eyes and kissed her again, succumbing to her touch, her look. He trapped her body against the cinder block hospital wall, reveled in the feeling of her firm breasts pressed to his chest, her warm mouth pressed to his.

She opened to him, her tongue tasting and teasing his as her hands dropped from his chest and snaked around his waist, pulling him tighter against her. But there was still an innocence about her, something in her kisses that told him this wasn't a common occurrence for her, either. And that she'd sensed the same unique connection between them that he had.

If he wasn't a prince, wasn't in a public place, he'd be tempted to pull her into a side room and make love to her right then and there. To act as any man but a prince had the right to do. He'd never felt such a connection with Lucrezia, or such an overwhelming physical need.

Damn.

He pulled back from Pia once more, his body giving an involuntary shiver at the unwanted separation.

Only a year had passed since Lucrezia's death, and nothing having anything to do with intimacy should be entering his mind. No matter how powerful the connection, no matter what the circumstances. What kind of man was he, kissing a woman when his wife had been dead and buried such a short time?

"I am sorry, Pia," he managed. "This…this is not appropriate."

"I understand." Her hands dropped from his waist. "I shouldn't have assumed—"

"No. It is nothing you have done. If I was any other man, I would not hesitate to—" Emotion gripped his gut. He didn't remember the last time he didn't have the right words for an occasion, or the last time he felt such abject embarrassment. "—to continue. I find you fascinating. But my life is not my own. I have obligations to my family and my country. People have certain expectations of me as a prince."

He couldn't meet her eyes. Instead, he focused on the bandage half-hidden beneath her hair. "And since Lucrezia…it is very soon. It—"

How could he say this? How could he make Pia understand? He wanted to kiss her, desperately. But he knew it went against all the rules his position bound him to follow. "It does not honor her memory."

"You don't need to explain. It's okay," Pia's voice was steady, but her words tumbled over one another in her haste to get them out, belying her nervousness. "We should leave, anyway. Your driver must have the car ready by now, and the reporters will be anxious to see you."

He swallowed, feeling he needed to say something more, to settle things between them, but all his years of etiquette lessons and experience in diplomacy failed him. He simply turned and began walking toward the double doors at the end of the hallway that led to the hospital's west entrance. Pia strode beside him, at his elbow. Just before he pushed open the doors, a laugh escaped her. He stopped and stared at her, incredulous.

"You are amused?"

"Well, at least I shouldn't need lipstick anymore."

"No, I suppose not." His mouth spread into a slow smile at her attempt to diffuse the tension simmering between them. However, when he looked past her, through the door's square, eye-level window to what lay beyond, he found himself working to keep the smile on his face.

At least thirty reporters, with cameramen at their sides, crowded the area just outside the hospital's revolving door. Behind the tangle of people stood two rows of news vans, most topped with blinding lights and satellite dishes.

"Here goes nothing," whispered Pia, her voice serious as she surveyed the scene beyond the doors.

"It *will* be nothing," Federico assured her. "I speak with the press several times a week. You need only stand beside me. My driver knows to make a subtle interruption and escort us to the limousine if anything goes amiss. But it will not."

The reporters caught sight of the pair as they pushed out of the hallway and into the lobby, then through the glass revolving doors at the hospital's main entrance. Immediately, the reporters elbowed forward, vying for the prince's attention.

"Your Highness!"

"How is Signorina Renati?"

"Can you tell us why Pia Renati is at the palace?"

At the cacophony of rapid-fire Italian, Pia stiffened beside him. He put a hand to the small of her back and eased her forward at the same time he waved for the crowd to quiet down and take a step back.

Once the throng receded and Pia was no longer in danger of being jostled, he removed his hand from her back. Keeping his voice well-moderated, he began, "Thank you for your concern. I have only a moment, however. As you might imagine, Ms. Renati needs her rest."

A familiar reporter from one of San Rimini's local news stations thrust a microphone forward. "Your Highness, can you tell us what happened this afternoon, and about the purpose of Signorina Renati's visit to the royal palace?"

"Good evening, Amalia," he greeted her in the light, practiced tone he always used with members of the press. "Ms. Renati is a friend of the family. She was playing with my sons this afternoon and suffered a cut to her temple. Thankfully, there is no permanent injury. As you can see, she has been treated and is being released." He shot the lean brunette reporter a grin and added, "Nothing more serious than when you had the dog loose in your studio last week."

Amalia nodded her thanks, smiling over the memory of the dog being showcased on their animal adoption segment that had escaped its leash midbroadcast, knocking the evening news anchor out of his chair. Happy to have her sound bite, she nodded to her cameraman that they could depart for their next assignment.

Another reporter stepped forward, one Federico recognized from the tabloid newspaper *San Rimini Today*. He gave the man a welcoming smile, but steeled himself for what would undoubtedly be a personal question.

"Your Highness," the fiftyish reporter stuck a tape recorder just inches from Federico's face, "isn't it true that Pia Renati has been living at the palace for more than two weeks? Certainly that constitutes something more than a friend of the family! Care to comment?"

A rumble went through the reporters, and they started shouting out questions again. Federico raised his hand for quiet while he wracked his brain for a suitable-yet-vague answer, but the crowd only grew louder. The reporter from *San Rimini Today* continued to waggle his tape recorder under Federico's nose, but worse than that, his questions caught the attention of all the other reporters. Even Amalia had perked up, and directed her cameraman to turn around and get a close-up of Federico's reaction.

"We understand your nanny, Mona Fennini, was dismissed today, though she has been on staff for only two months," the reporter raised his voice, making sure the crowd heard him clearly. "And you now say that Pia Renati was playing with your sons this afternoon. Is she being considered for the position of nanny?"

"As I said, Signorina Renati is a friend of the family."

Federico turned to another reporter, but the man from

San Rimini Today wasn't satisfied. In a voice loud enough for all the others to hear, he asked, "Then is there a relationship between you and Pia Renati the press should know about? A reason she was playing with your sons?"

Federico ignored the reporter, and asked others if they had any further questions. At the same time, he shot a glance at his driver, who recognized the signal and began to slowly pull the limousine forward, scattering the reporters at the rear of the pack.

"Your Highness, does Signorina Renati's presence at the palace have something to do with Princess Jennifer?" A woman he recognized from an Italian network piped up. "My resources indicate that Ms. Renati used to work for the princess at the Haffali refugee camp. The princess has not been seen in public in several weeks, and it has been rumored that she could be having difficulties with her pregnancy."

"And she did not accompany Prince Antony to Israel, as planned," added another voice from somewhere in the crowd.

Anxious to cut off any questions about Jennifer— and the state of her pregnancy—Federico shook his head. His voice adamant, he answered, "As you know, these talks began over a month later than anticipated. Princess Jennifer is now beginning her ninth month of pregnancy. Therefore she is keeping to a limited schedule and, like any woman approaching her due date, she is no longer traveling out of the country."

"Is that all?" the *San Rimini Today* reporter pressed.

"The princess had been making public appearances locally until shortly before Signorina Renati arrived in country. But on the day before Pia Renati's arrival, she canceled a fundraising dinner at the French embassy for her scholarship project with almost no notice. Is her pregnancy in jeopardy? Is that why Signorina Renati is here?"

"You have it all wrong," Pia's voice startled him. He'd encouraged her to speak English to him, giving him some practice at the language from formal events, so he'd never heard her smooth, San Riminian-accented Italian. "As His Highness has stated—"

"Isn't it unusual in your line of work to have so much time off? Or are you no longer employed by World AIDS Relief?" the reporter persisted, jamming his tape recorder under Pia's nose this time. "It seems like quite a coincidence."

Federico could see her expression shift as she scrambled for an answer. He turned to address the reporter, to rescue her, but Pia spoke first. "I've just wrapped up a project in the United States, and have not moved on to the next one yet."

"You're in between assignments?" The reporter's eyes brightened. "So you are technically unemployed—for the moment. Could this mean you're considering a position in the palace?"

"As a nanny to Prince Arturo and Prince Paolo, perhaps?" Amalia added, winking at Federico as if she'd caught on to a palace secret.

At that moment, Federico's driver came around the

side of the limousine and opened the door. Federico allowed the interruption, and waved to the reporters. "I apologize for cutting this short, but I am due back at the palace for a function. And I am sure Signorina Renati could use time to rest. I believe we have answered your questions to the best of our ability—if you have anything further, you are welcome to contact my secretary to schedule a separate interview. Thank you."

With that, he hustled Pia into the waiting car and slid in behind her. Once they were inside, with the doors closed to the reporters, he tapped on the sliding interior window to indicate the driver could depart.

"I was trying to help. Sorry if I said the wrong thing," Pia spoke in English again, turning in her seat to glance back at the scattering reporters behind them. "I thought saying I was between assignments would get them off the topic of Jennifer. I promised Jennifer...I didn't think...well, it just didn't occur to me they'd really think I could be your children's nanny. I'm supposed to start work in Africa shortly. If they'd done their research, they'd know that."

"It is very likely they do know. But they hope by pretending ignorance to obtain more information." Even as he answered, his mind was focused on her earlier words, which sparked an idea. She *had* been good with the boys. And he knew from palace gossip that she had little to do, besides keep the princess company.

Perhaps until he could find someone else...

He ventured, "The boys took to you this afternoon.

Surprisingly so, as they are quite tentative around strangers. If you were interested—"

"You have got to be kidding." Her eyes widened, then she added, "I'm sorry. That came out wrong. Your boys really are sweet. But Jennifer needs me."

She looked down as she said the last part, though, and he couldn't help but tease her. "You are bored, yes?"

"I never said that."

He pinned her with a look, and she raised a hand over her head to wave an imaginary white flag. "Fine. You've caught me. I'm bored senseless. It's not that I don't enjoy spending time with Jennifer. I do. She's my best friend. But there really isn't much for me to do. The pregnancy is tiring to her at this point, and she's not sleeping well at night—not that anyone could with a watermelon-size baby making it impossible to get comfortable—so she naps a lot during the day."

"Then you might consider—"

"No. Don't even think it. I would be the worst nanny in the world. And besides, I have a job. As I said, I'm due to travel to Africa in a few weeks. Once I'm there, I'll be incredibly busy, so a little boredom is probably good for me right now."

An edge had crept into her voice, and he could tell she was fighting to temper it. Was it because she objected to being a nanny, he wondered, or *his* nanny? After what had happened between them in the hospital hallway, it made sense.

But he'd never seen anyone able to put Paolo and Ar-

turo at ease so quickly. And with her years of experience as a relief worker, no doubt she possessed solid
organizational skills. She wouldn't lose Arturo in the
palace gardens or spend hours on the phone talking
fashion and boys with her friends, as Mona had.

He shrugged, though the more he thought about it,
the more the idea appealed to him. "It will be several
weeks before I can find a full-time nanny," he explained, forcing himself to sound casual. "I just thought
that, given how easily you related to my sons this afternoon, you might consider spending a few hours a day
with them until it is time for you to leave. Just to ease
your boredom."

She started to shake her head, but he cut her off by
adding, "It would distract the reporters from Princess
Jennifer's pregnancy. I did not think they would focus
on her pregnancy as much as they did. Their suspicions
will only worsen until the baby is born."

"I don't know."

"I would not consider you an employee. You are a
family friend, and—"

And *more*. That was the problem. If he was honest
with himself, he was asking her because he wanted to
spend time with her, learn more about her. He'd only
seen her once since she'd arrived at the palace, and the
reporters' pestering questions gave him the perfect excuse. In a few weeks, she'd be gone. Even if he could
never touch her again, just enjoying her company and
easy conversation brought him back to life, both in
mind and body.

And, if only for his boys, he needed to feel alive again. Feel an emotion, any emotion. Something to jerk him out of the passive life he'd been living. Perhaps then he could renew his excitement in his position and responsibilities.

"And?"

Her soft voice pulled him out of his thoughts. He shrugged, hoping he appeared nonchalant. "And I hope you will think about it. Next time Jennifer is taking a nap, feel free to come to my apartments and see the children."

He intentionally left out *and me.*

"Your Highness, Signorina Renati? We are here."

Federico blinked at the driver's words, startled to see that they'd passed through the tall, wrought-iron gates of the royal palace and were rolling through the gardens abutting the rear entrance.

"Do you need help getting back to Antony and Jennifer's apartments?" Federico hated for their time together to end. He still wanted to apologize for what had occurred in the hospital. At the same time, he desperately wanted it to happen again.

"I think I'll be fine. Thanks." Her color was high as she spoke, and he knew that she was thinking back to their kiss as well.

She let herself out of the car before the driver came around, smiled over her shoulder, then scurried up the stairs and out of sight.

Federico thanked his driver, then slowly ascended the stairs. Never in his life had he felt like such a fool.

* * *

"Idiot, idiot, idiot!" Pia groaned under her breath as she hurried through the back halls of the palace toward Jennifer's rooms. What was she thinking, kissing a prince? Or worse, making it so clear she enjoyed it?

He might have started it, but after he pulled away, obviously realizing he'd touched his lips to those of an idiot commoner who didn't belong in his circle—she proved that with her lack of sophistication with the reporters, if not with the kiss itself—she kept going after him like some lovesick groupie. A man with two kids. A man whose activities were public knowledge to half the western world. A man totally beyond someone like her, *if* she even wanted to be involved in a romantic relationship, which she didn't.

But holy romantic royals, what a kiss.

She tried to appear composed when she passed the guard at the end of the hallway leading to Jennifer and Antony's private apartments, but as soon as she rounded the corner behind him, she put her fingers to her lips, remembering.

Federico's olive skin had been as warm and satin-smooth beneath her fingertips as she'd imagined when she studied his face in the airport. His kiss, however, demonstrated far, far more passion than she would have guessed the ever-appropriate Prince Perfect possessed.

Why? Pia wondered. And just how much emotion bubbled under his stoic facade? Because she knew now, after seeing the concern etched on his face while the doctor gave her stitches, and after noticing the flicker of regret in his deep blue eyes when she'd mentioned the nanny, that he was a more complex man than the newspapers, and perhaps Federico himself, believed. He'd meant that kiss, body and soul. No one who still truly mourned a beloved wife could kiss like that. It wasn't possible. Even his words made it clear. He'd pulled back from the kiss because of society's dictates—not because of what he felt in his own heart.

But could he possibly be as blown away by her as she was by him? Could he feel the same connection she did?

Pia shook her head as she entered Jennifer's apartment. "Do *not* think about it," she chastised herself. Nothing would come of it, so why get her stomach in knots?

"Fine. Don't think about it," Jennifer retorted, causing Pia to jump. "But you have to know that I absolutely hate you right now."

Pia stopped just inside the door to Jennifer's bedroom and stared at her friend, unsure what she could possibly have done to make Jennifer upset. And ticked at herself for talking out loud, again. She hadn't mentioned Federico's name when she'd been muttering to herself, thank goodness.

Had Jennifer already seen the evening news? They couldn't possibly have reported her hospital visit so quickly, or the fact that Jennifer's pregnancy might be at risk.

Pia raised a quizzical eyebrow at the redhead. "You hate me?"

A smile lit up the princess's face. "Here I am, a contender for the title of Largest Pregnant Woman Ever, and you're standing beside Federico on my TV screen without looking the requisite ten pounds heavier. I hate you."

Pia rolled her eyes and laughed. She should have known Jennifer was teasing. But after today's emotional ups and downs, anything was possible.

"They already broadcast it?"

"They did." Jennifer clicked the television off, then tossed the remote to an empty corner of the bed. "Five o'clock news. Most of the local channels opened their broadcast right at the hospital, saying," she dropped her voice to a television announcer's tone, "Prince Federico diTalora and Pia Renati left the hospital only moments ago…."

Pia let out a deep sigh. "Well, quit hating me. The last thing I wanted to do today was end up on television. And I looked like a complete moron."

Jennifer's face immediately turned sympathetic. "I'm sorry, Pia. It's all my fault. I should have thought before I invited you here. At some point, reporters poke into everything this family does. And everything our friends do, unfortunately. I really appreciate that you stuck up for me." Jennifer screwed up her face. "I had no idea that the press was already speculating about my pregnancy."

"Don't worry about it," Pia waved her off. "But next time, wrap your own gift, okay? I'm no good at dodging boomerangs."

Jennifer nodded toward Pia's forehead and winced. "Does it hurt?"

"Not really. I've had much worse."

"I'm sure the boys are upset about it. They're great kids."

"I know. It was an accident, after all. I just… Jeez, Jen." Pia sank down on the edge of Jennifer's bed. "I didn't mean to get their nanny fired. I feel horrible." Horrible was just the beginning. When Federico had given the nanny that look in the palace hallway, just before he'd told the young woman to make other arrangements for the children's care for the rest of the day, Pia had been overwhelmed by her own memories.

At sixteen, she'd lost her one—and only—baby-sitting job. It was her one way to earn money and exercise some independence, to prove to herself and her mother that she could manage a job taking care of children. And she'd blown it, big time. The five-year-old girl trusted to her care had fallen off a swing when Pia had pushed her too high, landing hard on her back and shoulders. Those horrific seconds when Pia saw the young girl tumbling backward out of her seat, with her long brown braid flying over her head and her screams ripping through the air of the peaceful backyard—not to mention Pia's own feeling of fright—were forever imprinted on Pia's memory. As was the disappointed look the children's father had given her, which matched exactly the one Federico had given the boys' young nanny.

"Please," Jennifer nailed Pia with a look, her voice

serious. "You were not the cause of the nanny getting fired today. That's the third time in the last month Mona lost track of Arturo and Paolo. One time, Paolo wandered off and was found hiding behind a planter near the state dining room, which is at the opposite end of the palace from Federico's apartments. It's one thing for a nanny to let kids run around in a regular house. It's another in a royal palace where state business is being conducted. She was bound to get fired."

"It must be hard on the boys, though." Pia knew well enough from her own childhood, when her mother shuffled her from house to house. She hated being cared for by her mother's friends while her mother attended parties at all hours, sometimes far from home. Of course, Sabrina Renati had been required to attend those parties, as a professional event planner, but it didn't make the pain any less.

All Pia ever wanted during her childhood was a place of her own to run and play. And to have one person who paid attention and took care of her.

"Losing their mother, and now a third nanny, in only a year," Pia continued, trying to ignore the temptation of self-pity, "it's just awful. They really need some stability."

"I know. We do our best, all of us. Nick and Isabella read stories to the boys every single night. It's a ritual they've all come to enjoy. Before I got stuck on bed rest, I was teaching them how to play checkers. And Stefano has them all excited about a learn-to-ski program in Austria he registered them for this winter." She let out a tired breath. "We're trying hard. Federico's had a rotten run of luck with nannies. But the boys know they're loved, by their father most of all."

Pia nodded her understanding, at the same time she gestured to the television Antony had installed in the top level of the same antique armoire where Jennifer had her minifridge. "You mind? The six o'clock news will be on soon, and I want to see just how bad the press made me sound."

"Go right ahead."

Pia retrieved the remote control and clicked on the television. She took a measure of comfort in the fact that so many people cared about Arturo and Paolo, but a slew of aunts and uncles—or friends of the family— didn't make up for the fact they'd lost their mother. Especially when their father's job required such long hours.

"You know, the reporters actually had a good idea." Jennifer commented as the dramatic music opening San Rimini's evening news began to play and computer-generated graphics flashed across the television screen.

Pia dropped into a chair that afforded her a good view of the television. "How so?"

"About you being Paolo and Arturo's nanny."

Was this a conspiracy? A bona fide snort escaped Pia. "Maybe I can apply to be King Eduardo's secretary while I'm at it. Or, hey, how about Stefano's valet? He usually looks like he could use someone to iron his clothes. Just how many jobs are open at the palace? I can get my résumé together and—"

"I'm being serious," Jennifer countered, raising a pillow and pretending to throw it in Pia's direction. "You nearly exploded with joy when I asked you to wrap a present, just so you'd have something to do besides fetch me drinks or blankets or sit in the corner reading your umpteenth book."

"Didn't I just tell you to wrap your own presents from now on?"

Jennifer ignored the comment, barreling ahead. "I think you'd be a great nanny. Well, not a *nanny*. But while I'm napping or otherwise taken care of, I think it'd be fun for you to spend some time with the boys. They'd love it, and it would give you a chance to get outdoors and enjoy the sunshine." She rubbed her hands together, forging ahead despite Pia's protests. "I know! If you took them to the Palazzo d'Avorio, you could get some beach time in with total privacy. Only the royal family uses it, and it's right on the water. I'm sure Federico wouldn't mind."

"No way," Pia argued, keeping one eye on the screen as the weatherman pointed out current temperatures on his map of southern Europe. Early September was a fabulous time to enjoy San Rimini's beaches, but not as Jennifer suggested. "I'm the last person in the world who should be taking care of kids."

"You took care of plenty when we worked together at Haffali."

"No, I didn't. Most of them had at least one parent with them in the camp. I just made them balloons out of surgical gloves or taught them how to do cat's cradle. That's simple entertainment, which is a lot different than being someone's full-time parent. Or even a babysitter. I wasn't responsible for them."

"I don't see how playing with Federico's kids is any different than what you did at Haffali." Jennifer shrugged, her own thoughts obviously returning to the Balkan refugee camp where they'd helped reunite families scattered during the decade-long conflict in the region. "Of course you're right, and Paolo and Arturo have every luxury, while the kids we cared for were running from a war. But the concept is the same. Kids like to have someone spend time with them. And I know you're responsible. I've seen it up close and personal, under stressful circumstances, too." Jennifer hesitated. "Unless there's some other reason you don't want to be around the kids. Or Federico."

Bingo. Pia kept her eyes glued to the broadcast, unwilling to meet Jennifer's gaze. Jen would know in a second that something had happened between her and Federico. The princess had a knack for reading people's emotions, her friends' most of all. It was part of the reason Antony fell in love with her, part of what made her so well loved by the people of San Rimini.

But Pia wasn't about to admit to her attraction to Federico, not even to Jennifer. Or the twinge in her gut that made her wonder if she *could* handle Arturo and Paolo for an afternoon or two.

For all their rambunctiousness, the boys' sweet faces had touched her heart. And as Jen pointed out, it would get her outside, enjoying fresh air and exercise.

No, she couldn't possibly take care of them by herself. She'd need another adult along, for her own peace of mind, if nothing else, and that meant time with Federico.

But perhaps, if she spent more time around the prince, she'd realize how inane her attraction was. Any thoughts of having a romantic relationship with him—well, she may as well ask Brad Pitt out on a date.

Pia squared her shoulders and faced her friend. By the time she was scheduled to leave for Africa, she'd have Federico out of her system. No problem.

"I suppose, if it'll keep the press from asking more questions about you, I'll spend some time with the kids."

Jennifer's mouth spread into a broad, knowing grin. "Perfect."

Chapter Five

"I've reconsidered your offer."

Federico looked up from his copy of *San Rimini Today* to see Pia standing at the entrance to his family's private dining room. Her feet remained on the hallway side of the threshold, her fingers hooked tentatively around the doorjamb, but her I-hope-I'm-welcome smile made his morning.

He wondered how long she'd been standing there, debating whether to enter. The sun hadn't risen high enough to illuminate the dining room's interior yet, but he sensed she'd been awake for some time. Her clothes appeared fresh and unwrinkled, and her hair tidier than usual. Certainly more polished than she'd been yesterday in the hospital hallway, minus her lipstick.

He gestured to the large trays laden with eggs, bacon,

toast and fresh fruit that covered the table, trying to distract himself from the type of hunger thoughts of the hospital hallway—and her delicious, unlipsticked mouth—conjured.

"Please, join me. It was only put out a moment ago, and the cook prepares enough to feed the whole family, even when I dine alone."

Pia hesitated for a moment, then crossed the room and slid into a chair directly across from Federico. "Thank you. Jennifer ordered a plate a while ago, and it smelled heavenly. I get so used to eating whatever comes out of a can while I'm on assignment, I forget what real food tastes like until I return to the States, or come here to San Rimini."

Her eyes widened as she surveyed her choices. "I think this is what I miss most when I'm working someplace remote. Not movies, not television. Not even air conditioning. I miss hot, fresh food."

He couldn't help but laugh. "As you can see, I am quite spoiled. Though I admire you for your work in less than favorable conditions."

She said nothing, but he could see that his comment pleased her. He urged her to help herself, then watched while she poured herself a cup of coffee and added skim milk, skipping the sugar. The same as he took it. As she raised the cup to her lips, he found himself wondering what other quirks they might have in common.

He tore his gaze from her lips and directed a look toward her bandaged forehead. "How is your injury? I hope you are feeling better today."

She nodded, the muscles in her face visibly relaxing once she had a sip of the hot liquid. "Fine."

He swallowed hard and tried to mask the edginess she triggered in him by neatly folding the paper, careful to keep the headline out of her view, then placing it to the side of his plate. He wondered if he owed her surprise dining room visit to the tabloid's morning edition, which included a front page story claiming that "bizarre" events occurred behind the scenes at the palace this week, and speculating about Pia's involvement.

"So. You wish to reconsider my offer?"

"To visit with the kids," she clarified. She glanced at him over the rim of her coffee cup. "Play with them, keep them company, that sort of thing. At least until you find a regular nanny. Jennifer suggested I take them to the Palazzo d'Avorio, get a little sun and beach time for them and for myself. If they're even interested. They probably aren't."

He forced himself not to smile at her disclaimers. "On the contrary, I think they would like that very much." He started to pick up the paper out of habit, then thought better of it. Clearly, Pia was nothing like her cousin Angelo, who would have entered the room waving a headline that discussed his private life as if he'd won a prize. If she hadn't mentioned it by now she probably hadn't even seen the headline, so why stir the eddies of sexual awareness skittering between them into outright turbulence? If anything, he needed to clear the air. He took a deep breath, then plunged in, "Pia, about yesterday—"

"It's okay," she waved him off. "We don't need to talk about it."

"But I feel we must—"

"It was unavoidable. No need to discuss it, since it's not likely to happen again."

He opened his mouth, then closed it. Was she talking about the kiss, as he was? The boomerang?

Or had she seen the article?

She selected a slice of toast, forked some eggs onto her plate, then offered the tray to him.

"Then may I ask what changed your mind?" he asked as he took some eggs for himself. "About visiting with Paolo and Arturo, that is."

She shrugged. "I'm here to help Jennifer. I promised her before I even boarded the plane from the States that I'd do my best to keep the press from discussing her pregnancy, at least until either Antony's work is finished or the baby arrives. If playing with Arturo and Paolo keeps the press distracted and entertains the boys at the same time, that would be wonderful."

He took a bite of eggs, hoping she couldn't see his disappointment. She didn't mention *him*. Just his sons.

Not that he expected it, but he'd hoped, even if nothing could come of it. She flashed him a half-smile as she set the tray back in the center of the table. "And your sons really are sweet."

He had to laugh at that. "You do realize my sons are the same boys who struck you just yesterday?"

That elicited a genuine smile. "I do. They don't plan to hit me with a boomerang again, do they?"

"I hope not." He took a sip of his coffee before adding, "They received it just last week from the Australian ambassador. Though they have not yet mastered it, I do not possess the heart to take it away. So please, be careful."

"I'll know to duck this time."

"Good." He cleared his throat. "I planned to take the boys to the zoo today. However, I was not sure I wished to do so after speaking with the reporters yesterday. There is little chance we could visit undisturbed. And the weather today…what is the word for when the weather reporter predicts it?"

"The weather forecast?"

"Forecast," he relegated the word to memory. "Yes, thank you. The forecast is for rain. But if you have any ideas for activities, I should like to hear them."

Her coffee cup hit the saucer so hard he feared it would shatter. "Today?"

"Unless you have plans with Princess Jennifer, of course."

Pia regained her composure and shook her head. "She's planning to sort through her photos and put them in albums today, since she can do that in bed. I got everything out for her, so I think she's set. I just didn't think you'd want me to jump right in today."

He frowned. Jump in? What made her so nervous about a simple day playing with children?

Or were her nerves related to yesterday, despite her dismissal of what passed between them?

"It is up to you, Pia. But I would enjoy it if you could join me and the children."

"So…you have no official engagements today?"

"After I dismissed Mona yesterday, I rearranged my schedule so I could care for the boys for the next week or two. That should give me sufficient time to find a new nanny."

She sat straighter in her chair and lifted her chin a notch, as if resolving to tackle a difficult task. "All right. Let's plan something to do today."

"If you are certain." He hoped she didn't view spending time with him as an obligation. Why else did it seem she had to draw on willpower before accepting his invitation?

"Of course I'm certain. What did you have in mind?"

He thought for a moment. "Outdoor activities will not be feasible, unfortunately. Perhaps we could take them to the museum?"

"Kind of public, don't you think?"

"Perhaps, though not as likely to attract reporters as the zoo. Fewer photo opportunities."

"True. But Jennifer mentioned that she was teaching Arturo how to play checkers. Maybe we could find a new game to teach them. Something fun for a rainy day." Pia shifted in her chair. "My guess is the thing they want most is to spend time with you. Nothing formal, just a free day where they can talk and horse around, instead of going on some organized outing like visiting the zoo or a museum."

With a mischievous gleam in her eye, she added, "And speaking of formal, I'm going to teach you about using English contractions."

He stared at her for a moment, struck by a moment of clarity. She'd just hit on exactly the problem he'd had with his sons. Lucrezia had always given Arturo and Paolo plenty of free time. They'd sit in the nursery doing nothing in particular, or take long walks through the palace gardens. Yet ever since Lucrezia died, in his attempts to show the boys he cared for them more than his royal duties, he'd scheduled father-and-son activities for every moment of their time together. And worse, those activities were almost always in public.

The time had with them was limited, and he'd felt he had to make the most of each moment. But perhaps quiet time—private, unplanned time—was what they craved the most.

Pia's soft voice interrupted his thoughts. "I'm sorry. Your English is great, especially considering you didn't attend college in the U.S. like Prince Stefano and Princess Isabella did. I shouldn't tease you about it. And I really shouldn't assume anything about your children, much less open my mouth about them. I'm always putting my foot—"

"No, I appreciate your—" He searched his mind, trying to find the right word before finishing. "Your candor. In fact," he met her worried look with one that he hoped would reassure her, "I believe you are right. A day with nothing specific on the agenda might be fun."

They were interrupted by a staff member who cleared their dishes and replaced the empty coffee pot with a new one after refilling their cups. They each sat back from the table, allowing the man to do his job. Once he carried the last of the dishes into the kitchen and Federico and Pia were alone again, the prince leaned forward. "So, what type of activities *shouldn't* we plan?"

At an amused chuckle from Pia, he added, "English I can learn. But I do not believe I know how to *not* plan. I fear it is an ingrained habit."

"Well, I'm the expert of not planning. When we worked at the Haffali camp, Jennifer was the one who drew up each day's schedule and kept the whole place pulled together. All I had to do was follow a checklist and make sure all the important items actually got completed."

He leaned back in his chair. He wouldn't have guessed that, despite her usually scruffy appearance. "Knowing your mother's superior planning skills, I thought you would be the regimented one."

Pia flinched, and he knew he'd said something hurtful. Perhaps Sabrina Renati had criticized her daughter's managerial abilities?

Pia's voice was bubbly, however, when she responded. "You know my mother?"

"Of course," he replied, deciding to ignore the discomfort he'd sensed in her. "Our fathers were classmates, you know. When your father passed away and your mother opened her business, my father was one of the first to hire her to plan a party."

"I didn't know that." She fiddled with her napkin, then apparently realized what she was doing and stilled her hands. "I'm sure it helped her establish a good reputation. That was really kind of him."

"She earned it," Federico replied, and he meant it. "Sabrina is one of the most respected and in-demand party planners in southern Europe. My father and Antony continue to use her. In fact, the king hoped to book her for this weekend, when we host our annual ball to support juvenile diabetes research."

A vertical crease formed between her brows. "My mother is coming here?"

"Unfortunately, no. When my father spoke with her, she had already accepted an assignment in Berlin, arranging a three day festival for the German chancellor." A light laugh escaped him. "It is not often that my father is turned down. He was quite disappointed."

Pia nodded, but her gaze remained lowered, and unreadable. "I knew she wasn't at home this week, but I didn't know where she'd gone."

Her tone made Federico wonder if Sabrina's presence—or lack thereof—in San Rimini influenced her decision to stay with Jennifer.

Pia glanced back up at him, though the movement seemed to take mental effort. "I imagine the king found someone else?"

"He did." Realizing that she wasn't fond of the subject, he gestured toward the door. "The boys had a music lesson this morning. Shall we see if they are finished?"

Pia nodded and pushed back from the table as he said, "So, what *do* we do with them?"

"Have you asked them?"

He raised an eyebrow. "It did not occur to me. My parents certainly never asked me."

"Well, then. You might discover you like their ideas."

"I am not sure I like this idea." Federico rifled through Arturo's closet, searching for the boy's yellow rain slicker, and shook his head at the jumble of clothing. Even the maids were unable to keep up with the boys and their messes lately. Beside him, Pia checked the size tag in a blue slicker borrowed from his secretary.

Federico finally caught sight of a splash of yellow, wedged toward the rear of the boy's sizable closet. After fishing out the raincoat, he turned to Pia. "It is not considered proper for a young royal to run about in public in the rain. And they might catch cold."

Pia raised her eyebrows in surprise as she pulled on her borrowed blue slicker, then knelt to help Paolo thread one of his arms through the sleeve of his sunshine-colored one. "You never played in the rain as a child? Or splashed in puddles?"

"You have met my father, King Eduardo? No. It was not something he would permit." A lighthearted laugh escaped him. "And certainly not something I believed *I* would permit."

"But Papa, you said we could do anything Arturo and me wanted!" Paolo stared at his father in alarm.

"We're going, Paolo. Right, Papa?" Arturo shot his father a questioning look even as he stuffed his stockinged feet into a pair of bright yellow galoshes, intent on getting as far along in the process as possible before Federico could change his mind about their outdoor excursion.

Federico ruffled Arturo's hair. "I believe your grandfather has relaxed somewhat over the years. Perhaps, if I was a child now, he would allow it. And I gave you my word, yes?"

"Yes!" both boys yelled, giving each other high fives and nearly bowling Pia over in their scramble to get out of doors.

Less than five minutes later, however, Pia found herself agreeing with Federico. The boys' idea of playing in the rain might not be such a good idea, though she disagreed with Federico about the boys' catching cold. Rather, she suspected they'd ruin their not-made-for-serious-play outfits despite their rain slickers. Or worse, get hurt, given the slippery, rain-soaked grass.

The moment they'd exited the rear palace doors and taken the steps leading to the rose garden, Arturo and Paolo tore ahead of the adults. Pia feared one—or both—of the boys might tumble the whole way down, judging from the combination of their speed, the rain-slicked steps, and their tendency to turn their heads as they ran to see if their father was watching.

Paolo let out a whoop as he reached the bottom, then jumped off the final step, landing squarely in a puddle. Water and gobs of mud splashed onto his galoshes and khaki cargo pants. Pia glanced at Federico, expecting to see disapproval on his face. Her heart lifted, however, when he patted the pockets of his trench coat and cursed himself for not having his camera on hand to capture the event.

Arturo screamed with delight, also having gauged his father's reaction to Paolo's playful jump, then took the same leap off the bottom step, soaking Paolo with muddy rainwater. The boys kicked water at each other and held their hands out, trying to catch raindrops in their palms at the same time they deflected each other's splashes, until Federico reached the bottom of the stairs and urged them out of the puddle, onto a drier section of the gravel drive separating the palace from the garden. "Boys, boys! Shall we show Signorina Renati the swings?"

"Yeah! Come see!" Arturo skipped ahead, eyeing his father before skirting another puddle, which had formed in a tire rut. He yelled over his shoulder for Paolo to catch him, then made his way onto a smaller gravel path, this one clearly intended for walking, that led through the palace's formal rose garden.

"Are you prepared to run?" Federico asked Pia as he quickened his pace.

"Do I have a choice?" Pia took a stutter-step to catch Federico, thinking that while she was dressed for chasing children, in relaxed knit clothes and a slicker, Federico was not. He hadn't changed out of the tailored black slacks, gunmetal tie, and light gray button-down shirt he'd worn to breakfast. Instead of wearing a slicker, he'd donned a double-breasted black trench coat, far more appropriate for his usual government duties than for an afternoon playing with children in a rainy garden. She glanced down at his pristine black wing tips as he hopped another puddle then scooped up Paolo with one arm.

Good thing the prince was filthy rich. Those polished shoes probably wouldn't survive the day.

Pia jogged alongside Federico, who balanced a giggling Paolo on his hip. They allowed Arturo to lead the way along the twisting gravel path through the rose garden. Despite their rapid pace, Pia savored the refreshing sensation of the soft, warm rain against her face and the crisp scent of the perfectly manicured boxwood. Even the perfume of the roses, at the peak of their early-autumn bloom, seemed enhanced by the falling rain.

At last, they rounded a corner at the far end of the garden, where the boxwood-bordered gravel path emptied onto the palace's long, grassy lawns. As Arturo raced ahead, she realized a swingset had been tucked under the protective covering of two large trees. Evergreens dotted the surrounding area, creating a natural shield so neither those in the public areas of the palace nor those walking along San Rimini's cobblestoned streets, which bordered the property's wrought iron fence, could see the play area.

"You have so much privacy here," she marveled. "I didn't think that was possible anywhere on the palace grounds."

"You'd be surprised," he replied as he set Paolo down, then watched the boy follow his older brother to the swingset and hoist himself into a toddler swing. "My mother made a real effort to provide us with a normal upbringing. To her, that meant time away from the cameras. She selected this site. Antony and I practically lived in these swings as children. Later, Stefano came here—when he wasn't taking long walks through the gardens. Despite his reputation as a daredevil, the gardens themselves appealed to him more than the swings."

"What about your sister?"

He shrugged as he gave Paolo a push. "Isabella was quite the bookworm, even as a very young child. She always had a book with her when we came here, and sat on the grass reading instead of playing. Later, my mother encouraged Isabella to rummage around in the medieval section of the palace. I think, since Isabella was the only girl, and quieter than the rest of us, my mother wanted her to have a place of her own."

Pia leaned forward to help Arturo twist the ropes of his swing. When she let go of the ropes, allowing them to untwist, he shrieked with joy, then leaned back and stared at the overcast sky as it spun above him.

Pia returned Arturo's exuberant grin, but inside, she felt a stab of envy for Federico's upbringing. What she would have given for a hideaway of her own, as Isabella had. Or a parent who'd come outside with her, push her in a swing, or race with her along garden pathways.

She took a step back from where she'd been twisting Arturo and watched as the boy pumped his legs, driving the swing higher and higher. She looked sideways at Federico. He'd moved away from Paolo, who screamed that he'd swing as high as his older brother. "The queen must have been a wonderful mother to you," she commented. Despite her own wistfulness, Pia realized that Federico's loving upbringing probably helped make him a better father.

"She was. I still miss her. I was in college when she died—much too early." He lowered his voice, so Arturo and Paolo wouldn't hear. "I cannot imagine if I had lost her at the age my sons are now. My life would have been quite different."

"Your father would have worked extra hard to ensure you enjoyed your childhood," Pia assured him. "Of course, there's no substitute for having two loving parents. But I think, had your father been in your situation, he would have made the same effort you're making now. And you would have appreciated it, just as your sons will."

Federico nodded, the lines in his forehead a notch deeper, clearly pained by the knowledge that his children had been deprived of their mother. A yell from Arturo distracted him, and before she could determine the cause, Federico leaped away from her, lunging past Paolo toward Arturo.

To her horror, Pia realized that Arturo decided to leap from the swing—and he was far too high in the air to do so safely. Pia stood rooted to the spot, her stomach clenched in fear as Federico reached out for his son, breaking Arturo's fall just before the boy hit the ground.

"Arturo!" Federico scolded once he'd caught his

breath. "How many times have I asked you not to jump if the swing is so high?"

Arturo pulled a face. "I was four when you said that. Now I'm *five*. I'm going to be in kindergarten in two weeks!"

"It does not matter. You must never, never jump if your feet are higher than my head. You can get hurt. Especially on wet grass."

"I didn't jump, Papa! Look at me!" Paolo giggled and continued to pump his swing higher, oblivious to the risk Arturo had taken.

"Good for you," Pia finally managed to open her mouth and speak while Federico frowned at Arturo. "You're a very good boy, Paolo."

The little boy gave a one-sided shrug and grinned at her, happy he wasn't the one in trouble. Pia couldn't share Paolo's glee, however. The sight of Arturo launching himself from the swing, his legs kicking through the air and his arms splayed in front of him to stop himself from the inevitable fall forward, took her right back to the afternoon of her babysitting accident.

A hard knot formed in her throat. All these years later, she still hadn't overcome her inability to help, to prevent a child's accident.

Federico had moved with a parent's innate sense of protection, managing to keep his son from injury. Yet she'd stood there, unmoving, her heart beating so fast she thought it would burst through her chest.

Arturo gave his father a sheepish look that Pia suspected wasn't entirely heartfelt, apologized, then climbed back on his swing.

"Are you all right?" She asked Federico when she noticed he wasn't getting up.

He put both hands behind him on the grass and pushed forward. "Oh, I am quite all right. Merely annoyed. They never listen to me." He shook his head, but a smile played at his lips as he came to stand beside her. He dropped his voice to a confidential level and added, "At least not Arturo. I must keep an eye on him at all times. He is too much like my brother Stefano, I fear. Always testing, trying to determine how far he can push before he is disciplined."

"I think he'd give me a heart attack if he was my son."

"You get used to it. It is the nature of children." Federico took a step forward to help Paolo out of his swing, then boosted him onto the ladder leading to the short slide attached to the end of the swingset.

When the prince came back to stand beside Pia, he commented, "It is also their appeal. Everything is predictable in my life except the boys, and I take great pleasure in it."

Pia murmured her agreement, but privately, she wasn't sure she'd feel the same way, were she in Federico's place. Kids provided plenty of excitement without their tendency toward recklessness.

Still, her admiration for Federico rose a notch for his ability to appreciate his children's natural playfulness. How little credit she'd given him the day she'd arrived in San Rimini, daring to call his affection for his children into question. She couldn't have been more off the mark, and she'd been wrong to judge him by her own insecurities.

Arturo took a headfirst slide behind Paolo, then ran forward and grabbed his father's leg. "Papa, can we play hide-and-seek in the garden?"

"Only if you promise to stay within this area," Federico warned. "Do not go past the fountain. I must know where you are at all times."

Paolo's brow wrinkled. "We can't play hide-and-seek if you know where we are. That's not fair."

"You know what he means," Arturo rolled his eyes heavenward. "We can only hide in this section, and we can't leave it. It wouldn't be safe."

Paolo brightened. "Okay! Find me, Papa!"

With that, he took off, his steps awkward as he crossed the wet grass in his galoshes, with his slicker ending just below his knees and cutting his steps short. When he reached the edge of the nearest rose bed he spun around to face the adults. "Signorina Renati can hide too, *si?*"

"*Si,*" Federico agreed, then waved Pia ahead. "Go hide."

Whether the smile pulling at her lips was from relief at leaving the swings—and the memories they stirred in her—or at her amusement over being asked to hide by Paolo, who'd been so shy with her after the boomerang incident, she wasn't certain. But without a word to Federico she scampered after the boys.

Once they'd left Federico's line of sight, Paolo stopped running and looked up at Pia. "I know a really good hiding place. Would you like to hide with me?"

How could she resist? "Show me."

His brown eyes twinkled with excitement and he grabbed her hand. "Through here."

He led her down a side path, under a rose-covered arbor, then surprised her by pulling her around to the outside of the arch and onto a small patch of grass growing between the arbor and a row of boxwood hedges. "Papa will never look here," he promised.

"It's a very good spot," she whispered, wiping a drop of rain off Paolo's pink nose as they crouched low. "As long as you don't get poked by the thorns."

"*Si.* The roses are sharp. Look," he thrust out one of his tiny hands, showing her a scratch. "I got stuck last week. Didn't hurt, though."

Paolo leaned forward and poked his fingers through the crossbars of the trellis, careful to avoid the roses' thorny canes, and created a hole so he could see the path where it passed under the arbor. Arturo skidded by and made a face in Paolo's direction, clearly having had the same idea as his younger brother. Paolo giggled while Arturo looked back, listening for his father, then hid on the opposite side of the arbor.

"Mamma found this hiding place for me when I was just little," he whispered. "Signorina Fennini didn't ever find me when I hid here!"

Pia smiled at the pink-faced boy beside her, who obviously thought he'd grown from a little boy into a big one, but felt another pang of guilt over the nanny's dismissal. She wondered how much the boys had liked Mona. Clearly not as much as they adored their mother, though Pia found it difficult to imagine fashion-forward Lucrezia running through the arbor playing hide-and-seek, let alone crouching in the tiny space she and Paolo now occupied on the side of the arbor.

Still, she was glad the boys remembered their mother fondly. Even though little more than a year had passed since Lucrezia's death—and not long in an adult's memory—a year constituted an aeon in little kid time.

As footsteps approached on the path they'd just left, however, Pia's thoughts immediately turned to Federico. From her position, she could just see past the thick rose canes through a gap in the trellis. Mud spatters now covered Federico's black wing tips and the cuffs of his slacks, and she smiled to herself as he swiped a hand over his dark, wet hair. Federico needed to get messy, to cut loose and do something unscheduled, perhaps even more than his sons needed it.

And did the prince's blue eyes shine brighter in the rain, or what?

"Arturo, Paolo, Signorina Renati," the prince called out in a sing-songy tone she thought him incapable of, given his rich masculine voice and regal bearing. "Ready or not, here I come!"

Paolo moved closer to her, huddling up against her body and giggling. A tiny smile tugged at the corners of Federico's full lips, but he continued down the path, calling for the boys and pretending not to have heard.

He moved far enough past the arbor to be out of sight, though not out of earshot. She could hear him calling for the boys as he followed the circular path through the gardens, mock panic filling his voice at his inability to find anyone.

She glanced down at Paolo's excited face, flashing him a grin. "This is fun, isn't it?"

He nodded. "Are you going to play with us again tomorrow?"

"We'll have to see, sweetie." Aside from Arturo trying to give her heart failure when he'd leaped from the swing, she'd had a good time, just as Jennifer had predicted. And Arturo's jump hadn't been so bad, really. If anything, witnessing a few of the boys' daredevil antics might serve to show her that kids were more resilient than she'd been willing to believe.

"I wish you would." Paolo's face filled with a child's sincerity. "My mamma died and I really want a new one I can play with."

Pia started to answer, then clamped her mouth shut. How could she possibly respond to such a heartbreaking, yet innocent, request?

"Come on," Paolo grabbed her arm and urged her to stand, his thoughts obviously skittering from one idea to the next faster than hers. "Papa will return soon. We have to hide somewhere else."

"Is that fair?"

He shrugged, his eyes flickering with mischief. "Arturo does it all the time."

She shook her head in amusement, but followed him

down the path. His footsteps were loud enough as he crunched through the gravel that she knew Federico had to hear him running. She wondered how long it would be before he found them.

The idea of being found by Federico while she hid between rows of fragrant roses and boxwood, even though a child stood at her hip, sent her pulse racing.

She sucked in a deep lungful of the moist garden air, then exhaled. What was wrong with her? She had no right thinking about getting romantic with Federico. She had to start thinking of him as Paolo and Arturo's father. A man whose children needed stability, not an interloper coming in and getting hot and heavy with their dad then taking off for sub-Saharan Africa, where she'd be lucky to even have a phone, much less personal contact with him. Her whole goal in joining them this afternoon was to drive Federico from her mind, not to develop an even deeper crush.

Thoughts of Federico faded when Paolo took a sharp corner, bringing them face-to-face with a large fountain. Pia stopped short, her mouth opening in a quiet O. Never in her life had she seen anything so breathtaking.

A low stone lip separated the water of the pool from the path. In the center stood a large sculpture of an opening flower, with water shooting from the top in a hundred different directions. Statues of sprightly woodland nymphs graced each of the flower's leaf sets, spraying water down into the pool from carved vases, as if commanded by the gods. The water rippled with life, and she noticed several Euros and San Riminian draema along the bottom—wishes made by the royal family, their aristocratic guests, or their staff, who were the only people permitted in this area of the gardens.

"Do you like it, signorina?"

"It's beautiful, Paolo." Even with the rain, the sound of the cascading water brought a serenity to the garden that she wouldn't have thought one could find in the center of a busy European city. She studied the graceful arcs of water cascading into the pool for a moment before adding, "But didn't your father say that we shouldn't go past the fountain? Why don't we turn around—"

Where had Paolo gone?

She glanced toward the path behind her, wondering how he could have walked away without her hearing his steps in the gravel.

Then she heard a splash. When she turned and saw Paolo, her body chilled. "Paolo! *Paolo!*"

The little boy lay facedown in the water, his slicker floating out around him. Neither his arms nor his legs moved.

Chapter Six

Pia leaped over the low edge of the pool and jogged through the water toward Paolo's inert form, her heart thudding so hard she could feel it in her mouth.

Please, please, please, don't let him be dead!

She lunged forward, frantic with worry, though at the same time, realizing that he couldn't possibly have drowned so quickly. Just as she grabbed the back of Paolo's coat, he popped up, laughing and spitting water at her even as she screamed.

"Fooled you!" His face split into a huge smile, and his eyes sparkled with childlike delight.

Pia sat back in the water, soaking herself to the bone, and closed her eyes in relief. "Paolo, you scared me to death. Please don't do that again."

"Wasn't it funny? You thought I fell in!"

"Paolo!" Federico's voice boomed behind them, his commanding tone that of a prince used to having his wishes obeyed. "Get out of the water! *Adesso!*"

Paolo stiffened in surprise, clearly not happy to have his father witness his impromptu swim. He glanced at Pia, then waded to the edge, his face flaming as he approached Federico.

The prince's hardened expression left no doubt as to the seriousness of Paolo's transgression. "You must never, ever go in the fountain, Paolo."

"I just wanted to trick Signorina Renati." His voice hitched, though he managed to hold back his tears. "I was being funny."

"Playing in the fountain is dangerous, not funny. And," he slid a pointed look at Pia, which Paolo followed, "Signorina Renati thinks you're funny just the way you are. So no more tricks. *Capisce?*"

He sniffed, then shoved his wet locks back from his face. "I'm sorry I was bad, Papa. I won't do it again."

"Good. Thank you." He reached out to touch Paolo's dripping head. "You shall catch cold if you stay so wet. Playtime outside is over for today. We must get you some dry clothes."

"Do we have to?"

Federico needed only to raise his eyebrows to quiet further protest.

"Papa!" Pia looked down the path toward the sound of Arturo's aggravated voice as she pushed to her feet and tried to settle her nerves. "You didn't find me!"

"You must have found a very good hiding place,"

Federico praised him. "Next time, make it easier. I am not as good at this game as you."

Arturo's irritation turned to laughter, but Federico spun both boys back toward the rear doors of the palace. "Time to change out of these wet clothes. We have enjoyed enough adventures outdoors for today."

"Can we watch *Blue's Clues?*" Paolo asked. *"Per favore?"*

"No, Papa! I want *Power Rangers!*" Arturo pleaded, grabbing Federico's arm. "You promised me this morning."

"I think, since both of you disobeyed me today, that we shall skip the television. Perhaps tomorrow."

The boys grumbled, but kept it under their breath. Federico turned to Pia, his gaze softening as he offered her a hand. She took it, appreciating his firm hold as she stepped out of the fountain and onto the relatively dry gravel path.

"I am truly sorry, Pia. I did not think Paolo would ever…He knows better. I do not know what possessed him."

A need for attention, if she had to guess. "It's all right. I haven't had a good dunking in a while."

He frowned for a split second, then let go of her hand and brushed a wayward curl off her face, sending a ripple of desire through her entire body. "You should not have had a *dunking* today." He leaned back, raising his face to the sky. "The damp of the rain is bad enough."

"The rain's not so bad. It makes the whole garden smell fresh. And no one else is here. And it's nice to have the whole place to ourselves."

"That is true. I do not get time alone nearly often enough. Well, you understand what I mean." His blue eyes met her hazel ones, and a flash memory of their kiss left her speechless. He touched her cheek briefly, then took a step back, as if deciding their closeness might be too dangerous, then nodded toward his sons, indicating that perhaps they should catch the youngsters.

They walked side by side down the path, following the drenched boys back toward the palace. Pia tried not to think of how amazing it would feel to have her cold hand warmed by his larger one, or how exciting it would be if he pulled her under the arbor and kissed her as he had at the hospital.

No. She tried to focus on the path, the roses. Anything but Federico. Wasn't today supposed to cure her of her infatuation with the man?

"Today was good for me, despite the boys' behavior." Federico glanced sideways at her as the rear doors of the palace came into view at the end of the garden path. "Lucrezia and I almost never played out here with them. It has always been the nannies. Now I realize that was a mistake."

His observation surprised her. "Paolo gave me the impression Lucrezia played hide-and-seek here with him. That she showed him the hiding spot in the arbor." She found herself grinning as she added, "which was wonderful of you to overlook, by the way."

He smiled at the comment. "It is part of the game. But no, I do not believe Lucrezia played in the gardens with them. It was not…" he paused, selecting the right phrase. "It was not her style. She preferred to read or play quieter games with the boys indoors."

"Well, this was probably a nice change for them, then." She hoped she sounded diplomatic. If Páolo felt compelled to lie, or at least to imagine he'd played outdoors with his mother, then Lucrezia's death probably still affected the little boy more than Federico knew. Enough that he'd asked her if she'd be his new momma.

The prince cleared his throat. "I assume that you have read some of San Rimini's tabloids?"

What sparked that question? "From time to time when I'm in San Rimini. At the hairdresser, places like that. Not as a habit, though." She slid him a sideways glance. "Why?"

"Then you know that I am often called 'Prince Perfect.'"

She barely managed to suppress her grin. The look on his face made it clear he didn't care for the nickname. Hoping to put him at ease, she teased, "Oh, I think I've seen that moniker attached to you once or twice. Or was that about Stefano? With a name like Prince Perfect…" She pretended to think about it for a moment before shaking her head and asking, "Are you sure they meant you?"

She stared pointedly at the caked mud on his shoes and slacks, then tried not to laugh at the look of pretended pain on his face.

Unable to maintain his composure, Federico let out a roar of laughter, loud enough that Arturo and Paolo glanced back to see what caused it. Pia loved seeing the prince relaxed at long last. He put on such a stiff, formal front to the world, but underneath, she sensed he possessed a sense of humor and a tender heart.

"It most assuredly was not about Stefano," he said between laughs. "Only Stefano is convinced of his own perfection. And possibly Princess Amanda. But no, I do not believe that my present state of dress would qualify as perfect."

He swiped absently at a leaf that stuck to the side of his pants, then looked back to her, his features turning serious. "I despise that they call me Prince Perfect, you know."

"Why?" She hated to argue that, in her mind, he was the perfect prince. Caring, honorable, always putting others before himself—a whole country before himself. But if she uttered that opinion, he might realize the strength of her attraction to him.

Careful to choose the right words, she said, "I thought they called you Prince Perfect because you're the model of all a San Riminian prince should be. You know just what to say, how to act, and you've never once given the tabloids the slightest scandal to hang an article on. You're a perfect representative of our country, and I'm sure you've worked hard to maintain that reputation." She shot him an evil grin. "I bet it just drives those muckrakers nuts."

"Muck…? Ah, yes. The reporters. I am quite certain it does. But I am not perfect—far from it. I used to think I was, before…well, before. I prided myself on my behavior. But now, now I know better. For instance," his gaze flicked to the boys, who were joking with each other as they neared the palace steps, comparing the amount of mud coating their once-shiny galoshes. "I have not been a perfect father since Lucrezia died, and that is the most important role in the world. I thought I was doing the right thing, taking them on outings. Formal outings. But I felt off," he tapped his chest, "in here. Now I understand why."

He stopped walking, and Pia stopped, too, aware that he wanted her undivided attention. "I never realized how much Arturo and Paolo needed time just to be boys, with nothing to do but play. And to be able to do that with their own father, instead of a nanny."

"Well, you know now," she kept her tone breezy, hoping the prince wouldn't take himself quite so seriously. "And you'll continue to spend time with them, even after you find a nanny." A nanny who'd get to do all the fun things she wished she could do—play hide-and-seek, teach them magic tricks, build tents out of blankets…. She shrugged off the thought. "They know that. Today was too much fun to do otherwise."

To her surprise, he reached out and grabbed her hand. Despite the cold and damp of the palace gardens, his fingers radiated warmth and strength. "But I would not have understood it without you. Thank you."

"It was nothing," she replied, her voice huskier than she'd intended. Nothing that a lifetime of being ignored by her own mother hadn't taught her. Kids needed love. And time. Given his numerous duties, Federico might not have much free time—not an amount she'd consider ideal for a parent—but it was clear to her that he loved Arturo and Paolo with all his heart. He was a good parent to them, and he worked hard to make every moment of the time he could give the boys as special as possible.

For a brief moment, as Federico's fingers interlaced with hers, she wished she could do something special for them, too. Wished she could be Paolo's mother and hug away all his hurts, make him realize he didn't have to fake drowning or concoct stories about his late mother to get attention.

"It was something." Federico gave her hand a squeeze, then let go and began to walk again, unwilling to let the boys stand in the rain much longer. "You know, Pia, you will make a wonderful wife and mother someday. I hope your future husband and children realize their good fortune."

She forced herself to smile in thanks, but Federico had already jogged ahead of her to ensnare his giggling boys, one in each arm. Her insides went hollow as she watched them. How could she let herself daydream about him?

No, she'd never be a mother. Not to Arturo and Paolo, as Paolo'd asked. Federico's words—though meant as a compliment—also served as a dismissal of any potential for a relationship.

She mentally castigated herself for wanting him, then forced herself to concentrate on her steps across the gravel driveway, rather than on her emotions. Despite his passionate kisses, hadn't he said it was too soon for him? As much as her heart screamed for it not to be true, he'd apparently meant it. And after the way she'd flipped out when Arturo had merely taken a jump from a swing, or when Paolo played a simple joke....

She bit down on the inside of her lip. As much as part of her wanted to be a mother, to know the joy Federico felt every time he held his sons, she knew she'd never be a mother to her own children, let alone to the effervescent boys catapulting down the path ahead of her.

It was a chance none of them, least of all the children, could afford to take. They'd all end up getting hurt.

Why could he not keep his thoughts to himself?

Federico jammed Arturo's wet coat onto a hook with more force than necessary, then strode into the boys' small bathroom for a towel to dry their hair. He spent his whole life learning how to speak when appropriate, to hold his tongue when it would better serve him, his family, or his country.

So what possessed him to blurt out to Pia that she would make a man a good wife? It was entirely true, of course—Pia exuded a casual, friendly charm that any man would find refreshing. Not to mention her amazing sense of humor. But he knew stating it so boldly—that she'd make another man a good wife—would sound like a rejection, especially given the sexual tension that hummed between them and the mind-blowing kiss they'd shared less than twenty-four hours ago.

He'd done it to protect himself, he knew. To convince himself that nothing existed between them. But it did, and as much as it couldn't happen—he'd convinced himself that the mere appreciation of a woman constituted love before, and did not care to do it again—he shouldn't have pushed her away in such a rude fashion.

And then there was his comment about her being a mother. And the look that he'd glimpsed on her face before he turned away, running to scoop up the boys.

For all he knew, her edgy behavior at breakfast, as well as her look of dread when Arturo leaped from the swing or Paolo climbed in the fountain, resulted from an inability to bear children. He'd witnessed the same reaction among some of his friends who'd had difficulty conceiving. Invariably, they worried more about children's bumps and bruises than other parents, to whom children seemed more resilient, and were taken for granted. If not infertility, then something else sent her emotions on edge when it came to children. He had to know what.

"I am truly no Prince Perfect," he gritted out to himself. He'd hurt her doubly. No wonder she'd excused herself to return to Jennifer's apartments, despite the fact he had offered her dry clothes and dinner. It wasn't a desire to check on Jennifer, as she had claimed. He could see that in the way she averted her eyes, in the subtle drop of her shoulders.

And he'd heard it in her final words, when she'd reminded him that the boys still needed a nanny, then pointedly wished him good luck in his attempt to find one.

"Papa?" Paolo poked his head around the doorjamb of the bathroom. "Did you find the towels?"

"Si." He tried not to think about Pia as he fluffed Paolo's short, dark hair—so much like his own, yet with Lucrezia's eyes peeping out underneath. "Find your pajamas, Paolo, and bring them here. I think tonight you should have your bath before dinner."

"With bubbles?"

Federico pretended to have a hard time deciding, but a hug from Paolo made him smile. "All right."

"Papa, today was fun."

"I am glad you thought so."

"We can do it again sometime?"

"Of course."

"And will Signorina Renati be my new mamma?"

Federico's spine stiffened. "Why do you ask that?"

Paolo shrugged. "I liked her. She was nice. I told her I thought it would be good if she could be my mamma."

Oh, no. "You did?" When Paolo nodded, Federico asked, "What did she say?"

The little boy's mouth screwed up, then he replied. "I don't remember. I think we were going to the fountain and I forgot. Can I wear my frog pajamas?"

"Of course."

Paolo grinned, then ran off to find them.

He swiped Paolo's towel off the floor. He must have dropped it when Paolo asked his impossible question.

Good thing three-year-olds were easily distracted. But Pia would have a longer memory.

As soon as he finished bathing the boys, he'd have

his secretary contact the nanny service, as Pia suggested. But next time he saw her, he'd discover her secrets and apologize for his heartless comments.

As he'd told Paolo, the day had been too much fun not to repeat.

"You're soaked!" Jennifer's eyes were nearly as wide as her ever-spreading midsection when Pia entered the room. Pia took off her borrowed coat and hung it in the adjoining bathroom, hoping she hadn't already dripped on one of the apartment's expensive Oriental rugs.

Jennifer's gaze lit on Pia's wet hair and clothes. "I didn't mean that you should go to the beach *today*."

"We didn't. The boys wanted to play in the garden, splash around in puddles, that sort of thing."

Jennifer replaced the lid on a box of photographs, then swooped aside a pile of photo adhesive, scrapbook pages, and specialty markers to make room for Pia to sit on the bed beside her. Pia begged off, gesturing at her wet clothes. "I should change first. Thanks to Paolo, I got a bit more wet than I intended."

Jennifer smiled. "See, I told you you'd have fun with the boys. And I bet they loved it. Federico would never run around with them in the rain." At Pia's grin, Jennifer's jaw dropped. "*Federico* went outside with you? In the rain? You have got to be kidding! How did you convince him? Did he just die when he realized his designer suit would get wet? Or did he hold an umbrella over himself the whole time?"

"He didn't carry an umbrella, he didn't die, and he didn't need convincing. Not by me, at least. The boys said that's what they wanted to do today, so he went."

"Unbelievable." Jennifer dropped the photo paraphernalia into a storage box, then put her hands to the small of her back, massaging her muscles while she studied Pia. "Well, I suppose it's about time. He needed to do something relaxing. I swear, I've hardly seen him crack a smile since Lucrezia died. He's changed so much, it's hard to believe he's the same man I met when I first arrived here. I mean, he's always been the epitome of class and style in public, but in private, he's wickedly witty, and so kind—he even told a joke the first night I met him, at that fundraiser I attended here for the Haffali camp."

Jennifer shot an inquisitive look at Pia to see if she remembered her trip to San Rimini from the camp, then continued at Pia's knowing nod. "He made a crack about one of the countesses in attendance—a woman who, shall we say, was less than polite to me—just because he wanted to put me at ease. Given his public image, I never would have imagined…" She shrugged. "Anyway, I haven't seen that side of him much this year. Maybe the fact that he went out in the rain with you and the kids means he's getting back to his old self."

Pia tried to contain her surprise. While she'd seen glimpses of humor, she would never peg Federico as the type to poke fun at other aristocrats, especially those important to his family's social status. She wanted to ask Jennifer more about Federico's "old self," but a knock at the door interrupted them. Pia strode to the door, opening it wide to admit Jennifer and Antony's secretary, Sophie.

"Your Highness," Sophie nodded in deference, then handed the princess a stack of correspondence before turning to Pia. "Your mother just phoned. I have her holding on line three." She tilted her head toward the hallway. "I transferred the call to your room so you might have some privacy, but I can always redirect the call here, if you prefer."

Pia bit back her automatic urge to decline the phone call. Even Jennifer didn't know how deep Pia's frustration with her own mother ran, and now didn't seem like the time or place to discuss it.

"No, that's not necessary, Sophie. I was headed to my room to change into dry clothes, anyway. But thanks." Pia strode into the hallway and crossed to her guest room, just outside Antony and Jennifer's apartments.

She hesitated before picking up the phone, staring at the flashing red light next to line three. Had her mother seen the news report? Or had someone engaged in a little royal gossip and informed Sabrina Renati that her daughter was a guest of the diTalora family?

Pia took a deep breath, found a towel to protect the ivory silk-covered chair beside her bed, then sat down and picked up the receiver.

"Hi, Mom."

"Pia! I'm so glad I finally reached you. Why didn't

you tell me you were in San Rimini? I'm in Berlin, finishing up a project, but I can be there tomorrow—"

"That's not necessary, Mom. I'm really pretty busy here."

"So what *is* going on? I saw you on television with Prince Federico. I didn't even know you were acquainted. I realize that you know Princess Jennifer, but…Pia, is it true?" Sabrina's voice filled with hope, and Pia's senses instantly went on alert. "Are you seeing Federico diTalora?"

Pia stared up at the paneled ceiling. Trust her mother to be on top of every rumor in Europe. And to be thrilled at the idea of her daughter taking up with San Rimini's most famous single male. "No, Mother. I'm just here visiting the princess. No big deal, really. And I'll be leaving very soon for Africa. I have a new assignment. I just thought I'd stop by and see Jen before she had her baby."

"Oh."

"Don't sound so disappointed, Mom."

"It's not what you think, dear." Pia could easily picture her mother's exasperated expression. "I just want what's best for you. I want you to be happy."

"I am happy. I love my job."

"Trust me, a job is not enough."

Pia nearly dropped the phone. "This from the woman who loves her job more than anything? Look how much time and effort you put into it. You wouldn't do that if you didn't love it."

"I never said I didn't love it. But I put in the time

and effort because that's what it takes to be successful in this field. And that has meant a lot of sacrifices, as you well know."

An audible sigh came over the line. "I wasn't exactly a perfect parent. But these choices in life are difficult. Anyway, I had simply hoped you'd found happiness, that's all." Pia sensed a forced cheer from her mother. "I'll be back in San Rimini day after tomorrow if you want to reach me. Before that, if you change your mind."

"I'll let you know."

"Okay. You have my cell. And Pia, I do love you."

Pia hesitated before answering, "Thanks for your concern, Mom. I appreciate it. I'll talk to you soon."

After replacing the handset, Pia shucked off her wet clothes, leaving them in a pile on the bathroom tile, then pulled on a simple white shirt and a pair of black slacks, planning to return to Jennifer's room. After pulling a comb through her wet hair, however, she flopped on the bed and jammed her fists to her temples.

Why, why, why, did her conversation with her mother suddenly remind her of Federico and *his* situation? She shouldn't feel sympathy for her mother. Yet suddenly, guilt made her wonder if she should be more understanding—just as she'd grown understanding, and even appreciative, of Federico's struggles as a parent.

Maybe it was Sabrina's statement that she wasn't a perfect mother, that she'd had to make choices.

"Would have been nice if you'd chosen a career that let you be home once in a while," Pia muttered aloud.

Of course, a world of career paths hadn't been open to her mother when she found herself widowed with a young child. Sabrina had come from a lower middle-class family, and when she'd met her husband, had opted not to complete her studies. As the wife of an aristocrat, she only needed social skills, which she possessed in abundance, despite her meager upbringing.

Even Pia had to admit, the choice of a career as a party coordinator had been a natural one.

Just as Pia's choice, to help people in the far reaches of the globe, was a natural fit. She made life better for those who couldn't help themselves— refugees, the poor, the sick and children. It made her feel needed, and gave her a sense of purpose she'd never had during her childhood. And the more she could distance herself from her mother's high-society, busy-all-the-time lifestyle, the better. Or so she'd thought.

Pia sat up, rubbing a palm over her face. She pushed herself out of bed, and as she hung her wet clothes over the shower rod to dry, she resolved to call her mother when Sabrina returned from Germany. Even though Sabrina couldn't change the past, maybe now that they were both adults they could become friends. Or at least develop a healthy respect for each other.

Pia grabbed the calendar from her desk and jotted down a reminder to call her mother and invite her to lunch. She might not be able to work things out entirely, but at least she'd stop running from the problem.

After pocketing her room key, she strode toward the door. As flustered as her mother made her, another single parent plagued her thoughts. After watching Federico with his children this afternoon, she knew she'd only grown more attracted to him, not less.

If she didn't back off, she'd fall hard. "Too late," she mocked herself aloud. Good thing she'd reminded him that he still needed to find a nanny. If she spent another afternoon like this one, playing the role of nanny, enjoying her time with the children—and with their too-sexy-for-words father—the next thing she knew she'd be dreaming about having children with the man and living happily ever after.

Like Jennifer and Antony.

Now that she thought about Jen, however, Pia decided the princess had seemed more uncomfortable than usual. Her hands had been on her back while they'd talked, something Pia hadn't seen her do before. She opened the door to see if Jennifer needed her, but the phone rang before she stepped outside.

Expecting her mother, she answered, "Did you forget something?"

"Pia?"

Instantly, she recognized the voice of the director of World AIDS Relief. "Hi, Ellen. Sorry—thought you were someone else calling me back. I don't get many calls here. What's up?"

After a few minutes' conversation, Pia made her way back to Jennifer's room to share the news. It wasn't what she'd hoped to tell her friend. On the other hand, she reasoned, her Federico problem would be solved for her.

She couldn't exactly moon over an unattainable royal from two thousand miles away, could she?

Chapter Seven

"Federico. Federico, wake up."

The deep voice echoed through Federico's head as if shouted to him through a thick fog. He shifted to his side, away from the too-masculine sound.

"Mi lasci in pace," he mumbled, fighting to get back his dream. He'd been walking through the gardens with Pia, the children safely in the palace, and she'd been just about to tell him he didn't need to hire a nanny, that he should have his secretary call to cancel the interviews she'd set up in the hours after dinner that night.

But the gravel-edged voice speaking in place of Pia's jolted his slumber.

"I will not leave you alone." This time the voice was accompanied by shaking. Federico blinked, then jerked to sitting, realizing he was awake, in his private rooms.

"Father?" His voice came out harsh, tired, even to his own ears.

"I apologize, but I need your help."

Federico took in the king's clothing, the same midnight navy suit he remembered his father wearing to a formal dinner earlier that evening, then glanced at his bedside clock. Only 11:00 p.m. The boys must have tired him more than he thought, because he hadn't heard his father knock, and the king never barged in on his adult children. Despite being both their parent and their ruler, he afforded them a certain degree of privacy to encourage them to continue living under his roof, where high security could be more easily maintained.

"What is it? The boys?" Federico dismissed the idea before his father even answered, knowing he would have heard any disturbance with Arturo and Paolo first. He racked his brain for the cause of whatever emergency must have arisen. "Or are you leaving the country?"

It had happened before, when King Eduardo flew out to nearby Turkey after a devastating earthquake, or for emergency meetings with foreign leaders during the crisis in the nearby Balkans, but on those occasions Antony had been present, and he'd been the one awakened with the news.

"The boys are fine. I need you to take Princess Jennifer to the hospital. Signorina Renati sent word to me at dinner a few hours ago. The doctor says Princess Jennifer is in the early stages of labor, but progressing rapidly. I decided it best not to wait until morning for her to make the trip to the hospital. There are four tour groups scheduled to go through the public areas then, and she would have little chance of leaving unnoticed. No need to make the media scrutiny concerning her pregnancy worse than it already is. I'll stay here in case Arturo and Paolo awaken before you return."

Federico frowned, but pushed aside his covers and strode to his closet to retrieve a freshly pressed pair of black slacks. "You do not wish Antony's driver to take her?"

"He's not on duty at the moment, and I'm afraid of alerting the paparazzi if I call him to the palace at this hour. It would be easier if you could take your private vehicle and drive her yourself. Since my dinner guests are just departing, one more black Mercedes leaving the palace grounds shouldn't draw too much attention. Signorina Renati will accompany you, and will stay at the hospital until Antony arrives."

"He is on his way?"

"I phoned him before coming to wake you. He has my plane in the Middle East, so he will wrap up what he can tonight and depart at sunrise."

Federico located a pair of socks in the same jet black hue as his slacks. "All right. Will you need me here, or should I stay at the hospital with Jennifer and Pia?"

"I will call if you're needed. I had my secretary clear my morning schedule, and Isabella and Nick arrived from New York two hours ago, so if you feel the need to stay at the hospital, go ahead. The boys will be fine. I would enjoy having breakfast with them, and I know

Isabella is anxious to have them open some of the gifts she brought them from the States."

Opting for a casual look—for him—Federico removed a gray polo shirt from its hanger and wished he had at least a little time to shave and shower. Out of habit, he never appeared outside his room looking anything less than camera-ready. And then there was Pia. As much as he shouldn't care about impressing her, particularly in the middle of the night with Jennifer's baby about to arrive, he did. The fact that he'd dreamed about her—and awakened still wanting her—convinced him he wanted more than friendship from her. He glanced at his father. "I assume I need to leave now, or you wouldn't have come."

"Pia is helping Jennifer pack, so ten minutes for a shower shouldn't cause a problem. Apparently, the princess thought she still had a week or two to prepare for the baby's arrival."

"So did I."

A few minutes later, Federico stood in his Italian marble shower, cool sprays of water pummeling his head and forcing him back to wakefulness. As he engaged in a lightning-fast shampoo and scrub, he caught himself smiling. Come tomorrow, he'd be cradling a brand-new baby in his arms, a warm little body to remind him of the emotional births of his own children. It seemed like a lifetime ago that he and Lucrezia welcomed Arturo, and then Paolo, into the world.

He had to admit, as difficult as it was to balance his public schedule with caring for the boys, he would gladly welcome another baby into his home. He envied Antony that—and the love of a wife welcoming him back to bed with open arms while the baby slept in its crib.

As he shut off the spray and toweled himself dry, another thought occurred to him, this one far more practical. If Jennifer's baby turned out to be a boy, it would bump him from the line of succession.

Federico looped his towel over the appropriate hook and laughed aloud, realizing that for the first time in his life, he didn't care about the loss of prestige. The media offered Britain's Prince Andrew and Prince Edward more latitude once William and Harry were born, didn't they?

Perhaps, with an adorable child taking his place in line for the throne, and with attention focused on Jennifer and Antony as the world's most famous new parents, he could stop trying to be Prince Perfect and spend more time being a father.

Today had shown him the value of letting go, of reveling in parenthood, no matter what the media or etiquette dictated. *Pia,* a woman with no children of her own, had shown him. And tonight they'd get to witness parenthood's most wondrous miracle—together.

He wondered if seeing a brand-new child would affect her emotions as it had his. Or if sharing such an intimate event would draw them closer.

He pocketed his wallet and strode toward Jennifer's rooms, an uncharacteristic bounce in his step.

As long as Pia stayed at the hospital, he'd stay.

* * *

Pia forced herself to keep calm as she pulled Jennifer's hospital room door closed behind her, then made her way toward the coffee machine near the nurses' station. She needed a double, and fast. As unsettling as reading the pregnancy manual had been, watching her best friend ride through wave after wave of contractions made the pages of the pregnancy book seem as serious as a Peanuts comic strip in comparison. As with everything in her life, Jennifer faced the onset of labor with quiet courage. Pia, however, felt agitation creeping up at her inability to do anything but offer comforting words to the princess. She'd hidden her frustration from Jennifer, but a cup of coffee would help tamp it down further.

"How is the princess?"

Pia's head snapped up at the sound of Federico's voice, smooth and cultured, even at 7:00 a.m. "You're still here?"

Federico smiled, stretching his long legs out from under one of the narrow chairs lining the maternity ward's waiting room, just steps down the hall from Jennifer's room. "I called my father two hours ago. Antony is due to land at any moment, and I wanted to stay until he arrived, at least." He stood, looking her over. Tentatively, he reached forward and put a hand on her arm. "I know I asked how the princess fared, but I should have asked about you. You look…unwell."

"You can say it. I look like hell."

"No," he laughed. "Not so bad as that. Besides, I

don't believe I am permitted to say someone looks like hell. Quite a breach of etiquette for a prince."

"You used a contraction, though. You just said 'don't.' Even if you do fixate on proper manners, you're learning to loosen up a little."

"You see? Spending time with you makes me a better man. Stay a few weeks longer and I should be able to pass as an American next time I visit the U.S."

"Now you're getting ambitious," she teased, unwilling to test the seriousness of his invitation. "Walk with me to the coffee machine? I really need my fix."

"Of course. I would like a cup myself."

Once he'd fallen into step beside her, she commented, "I've been around pregnant women before, but it was always as part of the staff at a refugee camp, sorting out the emergency cases from nonemergency, and arranging for the pregnant women to receive medical care. Not *giving* it. It's different attending a birth in person, especially when it's your friend. And—" She shrugged, knowing her fear showed in her eyes, but trying to cover it by looking at an infant CPR poster adorning one of the hospital's cinder block walls. "I hate seeing Jen in pain, and when there's nothing I can do about it, and it's taking so long…I guess I'm just tired from being up all night, is all."

She flexed her fingers in an attempt to calm herself, then met Federico's worried look. "In answer to your original question, she's doing as well as can be expected with a first baby. I only ducked out to give the anesthesiologist room to work while he gives her an epidural. I'm sure once she's had some medication, she'll feel better."

She knew her words came out too fast, betraying her nerves despite her effort to keep them in check. Without a word, Federico pulled her into his arms. "It is exciting and frightening and overwhelming all at once. I know."

He took a deep breath, allowing his chest to rise and fall against hers. "But being present at the birth of a child forces you to reevaluate your priorities. To see what is important in life."

She smiled to herself, happy for his offer of reassurance after a long night without sleep, yet wary of what his protective embrace and tender words did to her emotions.

"How do women do this every day?" she mumbled against his chest.

"They don't do it every day. Just once or twice in a lifetime." A soft laugh rumbled through his rib cage. "Or in my mother's case, four times."

"I don't think I could do it once. Just being with Jennifer is enough."

He rubbed a hand along her back, his warm touch both a relief and a danger to her. "Sometimes, I think watching is worse than having the baby yourself. I was with Lucrezia when she gave birth to each of our sons. The first time, I almost passed out. One of the nurses had to bring me water. Of course, Lucrezia barely seemed to break a sweat."

She tipped her head back to study his face. "You can't be serious. You nearly fainted? *You?*"

"It's the truth. They even brought me one of those…I think you call it a basin?" The slightest blush touched his high cheekbones, and his grin turned sheepish. "I told you, I am no Prince Perfect. If I was, I would have stood there the whole time and held her hand without feeling anything but pride and excitement. Fortunately, the hospital staff signed a confidentiality agreement with our family, so my sickness never made the papers."

"I expect you were better with Paolo, though."

"I was. You will be fine with Jennifer, too." He held her tighter, and she couldn't help but notice how naturally her head tucked under his chin, how perfectly her arms fit around his lean waist. All too soon, he let her go, and she realized that Jennifer's labor and delivery nurse had approached to indicate that she could come back inside.

"Would you like me to bring you a coffee?" he asked.

"Princes do that?"

"When a woman stands in for that prince's absent brother, yes."

She grinned. "In that case, I take it—"

"Skim milk, no sugar?"

Pia's mouth opened in surprise, and his mouth curled into a self-satisfied smile. "I noticed at breakfast yesterday. I prefer mine the same."

Five minutes later, however, it was Antony who carried the steaming cup of coffee into Jennifer's room. He passed it to Pia with a smile, but his attention was riveted on his laboring wife.

"Why don't I leave you two alone?" she whispered to the crown prince.

He gave her free hand a quick squeeze and nodded. "I cannot thank you enough, Pia."

Jennifer, who lay on her side, clearly uncomfortable, but better for having the pain-blocking epidural, mumbled her agreement. Pia gave the princess some words of encouragement, then strode back into the nearly-empty hall.

"I see you have your coffee," Federico sipped from his own cup as he strode back and forth in front of the CPR poster.

"Yes. Nice delivery service. It's not everyday a woman gets two princes to bring her java." She exhaled, amazed at how he both calmed her fears and sent her body into overdrive with nothing more than a look.

The prince stopped pacing and tilted his head toward the room. "Any idea how much longer?"

"I'm guessing two more hours. Maybe three."

They both glanced at the oversize black-and-white clock suspended from the hallway ceiling, where the long hand jerked to click off another minute. "I have not yet purchased a gift for the baby. Perhaps we can make a quick visit to the gift shop? It should open soon."

Pia nodded her agreement and gestured for Federico to lead the way. They left the maternity ward and entered the waiting elevator, each acutely aware of each other's presence in the confined space. Seconds later, the lift stopped on the floor below to admit a tired-faced girl in a wheelchair. The nurse pushing the chair hesitated at seeing the prince, but he waved her in, holding the door open until the child was safely inside.

"Are you Prince Federico?" Excitement laced the girl's voice as she realized who stood before her.

Crouching down so she could get a better look at his face, he replied, "I am. What is your name?"

"Carlotta."

"That's quite beautiful." He angled a look at the cast on her leg. "It looks like you broke your leg, Carlotta."

"I fell off the balance beam. I had surgery yesterday to fix it."

He touched her arm, pretending to feel a muscle. "You are a strong girl, Carlotta. I think you will be back at gymnastics again very soon." The doors closed, and after the nurse punched the appropriate button, he leaned forward to whisper to Carlotta in a voice just loud enough for Pia and the nurse to hear, "I know you probably want all your friends to sign it first, but may I sign your cast?"

"Would you? Really?"

"I would be happy to." The nurse handed Federico a pen from her jacket pocket, and he signed the cast in quick, fluid strokes. The doors opened on the girl's floor, and Federico handed the nurse her pen. "Get well soon, Carlotta. And make sure you're very good for your nurse."

"I will!"

The nurse beamed and thanked him as she wheeled her charge out of the elevator, then both nurse and patient looked back over their shoulders and waved before the doors slid closed once again.

Federico turned to Pia and started to say something, then closed his mouth and reached toward the corner of her eye. "What is this?"

Pia blinked in shock, realizing that he'd just wiped away a tear. She almost told him she had dirt in her eye, but he'd know it for a lie. "You must think I'm the world's biggest wimp."

"Why would you say that?" A look of genuine puzzlement crossed his face.

"Well, first, I'm barely holding it together in there for Jennifer. Then I nearly lost it yesterday when Paolo made his little fountain joke. And that girl…the way you made her day was so sweet." Embarrassment caused her cheeks to heat. "I'm not this way all the time, really."

"I do not think you could work with refugees, or with AIDS patients, if you did not possess a great deal of fortitude."

"It's just kids." She knew she was babbling, but couldn't stop. "I've never been very good with them, and when I see them hurting, like that little girl—"

"Now you're the one joking, right?"

"'Fraid not."

"Well, you have been wonderful with Arturo and Paolo." His features softened, and Pia marveled at how Federico's love of his sons radiated from him as he spoke. "Not only yesterday, in the garden, but when they hit you with the boomerang. Many adults would have chastised them, or at least given them nasty looks. You went out of your way to make them feel *better* about themselves. You realized how upsetting it was to them, and despite your injury, you made the effort to comfort them."

He shrugged as they exited the elevator, then turned left, following the signs on the hospital's ground floor toward the gift shop. "You have a natural skill with children. And with adults, as well. The nurse who came out of the princess's room a few hours ago told me that Jennifer was holding up better than expected for her first labor and delivery, since she had you to keep her company. You were rubbing her back, helping her with her breathing...I don't think you give yourself enough credit."

He paused, waiting for her to meet his gaze. When she did, the intensity of his blue eyes and his serious expression rendered her motionless.

"Federico?"

"I wanted to tell you...I was wrong yesterday. When I made that comment as we left the garden with Paolo and Arturo."

"What comment?"

"That you would make a good wife and mother for someone."

She laughed and continued walking, hoping he couldn't see how even his mention of the terms "wife and mother" affected her. "You're apologizing for that? It was a nice compliment. Unless, of course, you didn't mean it."

"No." He touched her shoulder, stopping her. "It was wrong, after what happened the last time we were here, in the hospital. After I kissed you. What I really was thinking was that you would make a wonderful wife for me. And mother to my children." Pia fought not to show her shock, or her pleasure, wrong as it was, at his words. He continued, "It felt so easy, playing in the rain with the boys. I—I have never felt that relaxed before. So comfortable with a woman, and with my children. Yet it was not simply *comfortable.* I was always comfortable with Lucrezia, but yesterday, there was something more. I could not help but wonder if we…"

Pia clenched her coffee cup tighter to steady her hands. Federico diTalora, the man every woman in the Western world wanted, found "something more" with *her?* A woman who couldn't tell Prada from Gucci even on pain of death?

Impossible. And so, so wrong for her. Still, she had to know, had to hear him speak the words. "We—?"

"I do not mean now, obviously." Emotion colored his speech, and for the first time since meeting him, Pia wondered if Federico experienced nervousness. "I was sincere when I said that I feel I must honor Lucrezia. She was my dearest friend. But if I was to marry again, well…I would hope it would be to a woman like you."

He reached out and touched her hand, his fingers moving over hers. Though his touch was gentle, no one who noticed them standing near the doors to the hospital gift shop would mistake the connection for anything but a romantic one. "How does a man who has two small children, and who lives his whole life before cameras, ask a woman if she might consider spending time with him?"

Pia could do nothing more than stare at the prince, riveted both by what he said and by the bare desire simmering in his gaze. Words refused to pass her lips, but Federico relieved her of the need to speak by tossing his coffee cup into a nearby garbage can and pulling her slowly away from the gift shop. Hand in hand, they made their way back down the hall in silence, desperate to escape the curious stares of patients, visitors and staff who would occupy the halls as the morning wore on. Without warning, he pulled her into a small office, shut the door behind them, then flipped the dead bolt.

"This belongs to our family doctor." Federico's voice came out barely above a whisper as he took Pia's coffee cup from her free hand and reached past her, brushing his upper body against hers, to set it on the desk. "I shall have to remind him to keep it locked."

"I think he came to the hospital earlier to inquire about Jennifer," Pia managed, though having her fingers still intertwined with Federico's and his model-worthy face only a breath away from hers muddied her thoughts. There was only one reason he'd bring her in here.

She turned her head just enough to study the room. The fluorescent lights of the hallway filtered through the door's smoky glass, casting the room in a diffused half-light. Patient files filled an in-box on one side of the desk, but otherwise the room was clean and neat. She took a half step back from him. As much as her body sensed the inevitable, and welcomed it, her brain continued to fight. "If he left it unlocked, it probably means he'll be back—"

"He left the maternity ward an hour ago and took his car keys with him," Federico ground out even as turned Pia's head so her mouth met his.

Need and frustration warred within her as his soft lips brushed hers, and she realized that for the first time since they met no one could interrupt them—no kids, no photographers, no palace staff. Unable to resist the temptation, she returned his kiss. The warmth of his large hands on her back, pulling her body hard against his own, dashed any ability she had to protest, to tell him that she'd already received the call to leave San Rimini, and that long before that, she'd learned she'd never be the right fit for a man like him.

A low groan came from the back of his throat, causing her to melt in response.

What was the harm in a simple kiss, really? She'd already realized she'd never get him out of her system. Since the last time they'd kissed, he'd filled her every waking thought. Nothing too intense could happen in a public hospital, so why not just grab one more memory? Something to dream about the next time she found herself working in a dusty field, helping get water for a small village, or sitting in a stifling hut, talking to women about AIDS prevention?

She opened her mouth to his, tasting a hint of coffee as he slowly eased her toward the desk. In the nick of time, she broke the kiss and moved the coffee cup he'd left near the edge of the blotter. Then, running her hands in slow, worshipful patterns across his broad chest and arms, she nearly died to find firm, perfectly proportioned muscle beneath her fingertips. Despite his tightly regimented life, Federico obviously found time for exercise—lots of it, judging from the way his shoulders strained the cotton of his gray polo shirt, showing off his physique in a way his suits never could.

"When—"

"Five in the morning," he whispered, reading her mind. "Before the boys are awake. It is the only time I have completely to myself."

How much was there to discover about him? And how much would she regret the decision she had to make, to go back to work in Africa? Still, she knew it had to be done.

He bent to capture her lips again, teasing, pulling, nipping. His beautiful, warm mouth eased over to kiss the tender spot where her jaw met her ear, then drifted downward, kissing the column of her throat with a heat that left her mind reeling. He lifted her onto the desk, and without thinking, she wrapped her legs around his waist, her arms around his broad, powerful back. What would she do to have this man naked in her bed? *And how amazing would it be?* a dangerous part of her mind contemplated.

His hands tangled in her hair, and when he raised his head, glazed, sultry eyes met hers. He leaned in to take her mouth with his once more, but hesitated, kissing her cheek instead, then turning to whisper in her ear.

"Does this mean you will consider staying?"

Chapter Eight

Federico pulled back when she didn't answer, noticing the flicker of wariness in her eyes. "For a while," he clarified. "And *not* as a nanny to my sons. Do we not owe it to ourselves to see where this leads?"

Unless she didn't want to, he almost added. Had he moved too quickly? He'd never dated before—never a woman of his choosing, at least. Perhaps, overcome by the sense of adventure she had stirred in him, he'd gone about it incorrectly.

"I can't." Her eyes clouded and her expression went blank, unreadable. "But it's not you, Federico. It's me."

He dropped his hands from her waist and forced a smile to his face, though he knew it didn't reach his eyes. "I have seen enough American film to know that is what you call a 'polite brush-off,' yes?"

"No, no. It's just…my supervisor called last night from D.C. I can't stay. I'm supposed to go to my next assignment a week from today."

"If you did not wish to go, you could postpone it."

She opened her mouth, but he responded for her. "But you do not wish to stay. It is all right." He turned toward the door, but her touch on his arm stopped him.

"I'm sorry, Federico. You have no idea…" Her eyes brightened, but she blinked back the tears before they could spill. "I want to give this a try, more than you know. I just can't. In the long run, I'd be doing you a disservice by staying."

Lucrezia. It had to be Lucrezia. He shook his head, then turned to sit on the desktop beside her. He wasn't a man to discuss his personal life with others. Not only was he reserved by nature, but such indiscretion posed a great risk to someone of his birthright. However, if he didn't explain himself now, he might never find the happiness that Antony, Stefano, or Isabella had in their lives.

In taking Lucrezia from him—as painful as it was— fate afforded him a second chance. He couldn't let it pass. But could he explain that without sounding heart-less?

His only option was to tell Pia everything, and hope for the best. "Pia, there is something we must straighten out between us." He took a deep breath, then continued, "I allowed you to believe an untruth about me when I picked you up at the airport, the day you arrived in San Rimini."

She frowned. "What?"

"I did not wish for them to marry." At her look of confusion, he added, "Antony and Jennifer. When Antony first considered pursuing Jennifer, I told him I did not believe they should marry."

Pia raised her hip higher on the desk and looked at him in astonishment. He could tell she remembered their conversation in the limousine, when she'd made an offhanded comment about how she couldn't believe that Jennifer and Antony were married, let alone about to become parents.

"Why not?"

"I felt that a prince should marry someone of stature, of an aristocratic family. Someone who understood our country and its traditions, someone who understood the role Antony was destined to fulfill as king. I did not believe an untitled woman—an American, and a relief worker—could possibly do that, despite the fact I had met Jennifer and admired her. And despite the fact that I knew Antony had…" he drifted off, tapping his chest.

"Given her his heart?" she asked softly.

"Yes. It was apparent to me from the first time I met Jennifer at a palace function, when I saw that my brother's eyes never left her, how he felt. She tested him, made him reconsider his goals and his desires. She treated him as a man, not a prince. And he loved her for it."

Pia seemed to wrestle with the information, her gaze focused on his jaw, then lifting to study his eyes, to evaluate his seriousness. "Why are you telling me this?"

"Because I was mistaken in my original assessment. Antony could not have found a better bride, a better mother for his children or a better woman to someday become San Rimini's queen." Federico sucked in a deep breath, then glanced toward the door. Somewhere, several floors above them, Antony and Jennifer were about to become parents. Their love for each other would only grow as their family grew, unlike what happened in his own marriage. Nothing had changed between him and Lucrezia.

He returned his focus to Pia. "If I was mistaken about Princess Jennifer, perhaps I was mistaken in other things." He reached over to caress her shoulder. "I know I was mistaken to marry Lucrezia. I knew it the day she died, when I saw that Stefano was going to give up marrying Amanda and follow my father's suggestion of an arranged marriage, like mine."

"Stefano and Amanda—?"

He waved off her confused look. "It is a long story. My point is that on the day Lucrezia died, I realized that I robbed her of the chance to live her life with another, with someone who truly loved her. I told Stefano not to make the same mistake." Squeezing Pia's hand, he added, "But it was only yesterday, when I enjoyed our day in the garden, and the freedom of playing with my children as I was meant to, that I finally understood marrying Lucrezia was a mistake for *me,* as well. I robbed myself of an opportunity, I did not simply rob Lucrezia of one."

"You married her, but you weren't in love?" Pia's voice cracked on the last word.

He shook his head. "I loved her, in a way. But I was not *in* love with her. She was my best friend, someone I had known and understood since childhood. I married her because I knew it was good for San Rimini, because I was told from birth that I must marry well, and produce heirs so the diTalora family would remain on the throne and our nation would remain politically stable, despite the conflicts in the Balkans and the corruption in neighboring governments."

At the look of doubt on Pia's face, he added, "Do not mistake me. We got along well, and I miss her every day. But there was no passion in our marriage."

Pia's words were measured, careful. "Would you do it over again, though? Your royal duties are important to you. Not to mention your family and your nation."

He eased off the desk so he stood before her, looking her straight in the eye. He needed to drive home the importance of his words. "No, and not only because I was wrong to cheat Lucrezia. Because I followed my duty and ignored my heart's desires, I missed the opportunity to marry someone like you. Someone who treats me with respect, who speaks to me as if I was any other human being and not a prince. Someone who appreciates my children, and whom they appreciate in return. Someone who cares for her friends, who can handle any crisis and who cares about those who cannot help themselves. I cheated myself out of what Antony and Jennifer share." He captured her chin with his palms. "Pia, I believe we could share such a love.

A passionate love. But not if you leave, and we deny ourselves the opportunity to discover it."

He dropped his hands and massaged her fingertips with his, marveling at the lives she'd improved. How many times had her hands directed an elderly refugee to shelter for the night? How often had they served food to the hungry and the poor?

How could he have ever thought her scruffy and brash when she was far closer to perfect than he'd ever be?

"I believe," he met her gaze again, "that you are even more bound to duty than I. This is why you go to Africa, rather than pursuing your heart's desire. By following your duty, you could make the same mistake I once made. Do you not think so?"

To his shock, she shook her head. He'd expected happiness, a "perhaps you're right." Instead, her jaw trembled and she refused to meet his gaze.

"I think," she whispered, "they call you Prince Perfect because you see the goodness in others, even when it isn't there." She touched her index finger to her lips, then to his. Pain filled her eyes at their simplest of kisses. "I'm not that noble, Federico. I'm going to Africa because I'm simply not strong enough to stay here."

She slid off the desk and brushed past him, flipping open the dead bolt on the door. She started to walk out, but stopped for a moment. "Why don't you go to the gift shop. I'll meet you in Jen's room. She'll want me there when the baby arrives. Then we can go our separate ways and do what's best in the long run."

With that, she turned and strode toward the elevators.

* * *

Pia collapsed against the cold metal wall of the elevator the second the door closed behind her, hiding her from the world. Using the flat of her hand, she swiped away her tears then dried them on her slacks. Why did Federico have to be so damned…so damned *perfect?*

How could she be so *not?*

She'd allowed herself to kiss him because—deep in her heart—she believed he'd never be serious about her. A man still in mourning for his beloved wife was nothing more than a man on the rebound, one who'd forget her before her plane even landed in Africa.

But apparently, Federico wasn't a man on the rebound. He was a man discovering love for—quite possibly—the first time. As much as the thought overjoyed her, if she stayed, knowing that she could never truly give herself to him, then she was treating him no better than he'd treated Lucrezia.

Worse, even.

Pia swallowed against a fresh bubble of sorrow before it broke to the surface and made her cry again. Jennifer needed her now. Before facing her friend—or holding Jennifer's child—she had to forget what Federico had said. The last thing she needed to do right now was lose her concentration when an infant, especially one so tiny, rested in her clumsy arms.

She might have fallen in love with Federico—no, she *knew* she'd fallen in love with him, even before he pulled her into the office to kiss her, before he told her the truth about his marriage—but her own demons were stronger. More dangerous. If she allowed herself to succumb to him, to pretend to him and to herself that she could be everything he wanted her to be, his children would be hurt. Maybe not tomorrow, or the next day, but eventually.

How could she do that to them when hundreds of other women, women who'd make far better mothers, would marry Federico in a heartbeat?

As she left the elevator on the maternity level, a roar of cheering reached her ears. Within seconds, she turned the corner near the waiting room to see giant clusters of blue balloons tied to the nursing station, compliments of the medical staff, who'd apparently had them hidden away waiting for the royal infant's arrival. Curious doctors and nurses filled the hall, slapping each other on the back, hugging and singing.

Jennifer had sailed through the end of her labor and delivered a healthy baby boy—a future king.

When Pia managed to make her way through the ready-to-party staffers and reached Jennifer's door, a genuine smile lit her face at the scene inside.

How could her demons be so incredibly cute?

Federico halted just outside the door to Jennifer's room at the sight of his sister-in-law finally slumbering. Beside her, on an uncomfortable-looking chair, Antony shifted, half asleep. Federico took a cautious step inside, hoping to see Pia, to lure her out, but the room was empty save the royal couple.

Federico turned to leave, but stopped at the sound of

Antony gently clearing his throat, hoping to catch his attention without waking Jennifer.

"All well?" Federico mouthed.

Antony nodded, straightening in the chair and gesturing Federico back inside. In a whisper, the crown prince explained, "My son is across the hall, in the nursery. He just had his first bath."

Federico grinned at the pride in his older brother's voice. "And Enzo is as tired as his mother, yes?"

Antony nodded. "It has been a long day for all of us. I have not checked on him for an hour or so. I hoped you might—"

"Of course. You rest. You will have much to keep you busy when you return to the palace." He cocked his head toward the window, where several stories below, a cadre of reporters from around the world waited for the chance to speak with Antony. "Not only with a new baby, but with the reporters and with the Middle East crisis negotiation."

"I know all too well." Antony took a deep breath and nodded, put a hand on the bed beside his sleeping wife, then leaned back in his chair and closed his eyes, savoring his first hours as a parent.

Federico backed out of the room, fighting back the wave of jealousy washing over him.

He could easily envision having the same life with Pia, given some time. Lying next to her, their heads side by side on their pillows after the boys were asleep, discussing what adventures the next day might hold. Tucking her wild blond hair back from her face to look into her soft hazel eyes and kiss her good-night, or to awaken her in the morning. Watching over her, caring for her as Antony did Jennifer.

He grunted to himself as he walked toward the nursery. Not only did he find Pia physically beautiful, with her fair skin and not-quite-polished look, which was one hundred and eighty degrees from the wealthy, pampered women who tended to frequent his life. But Pia, when she relaxed, showed a sharp wit, a heart so big she wanted to aid the world, and an intellect that would challenge him every day of his life.

As much as he thought he'd never want another woman in his life after the disaster he had created by marrying Lucrezia, he wanted Pia. Desperately. And this time, he wouldn't worry about public opinion.

He muttered in frustration. He knew she was attracted to him, as well—she'd as much as admitted it. Besides, no woman had ever kissed him as she did, with such passion.

But what frightened her so deeply?

He hated the look of panic he'd seen cross her face when he'd returned to Jennifer's room from the gift shop with a large stuffed bear under each arm—one for the baby, one for the mother. He'd been stunned to see that Jennifer had already given birth, but not so distracted that Pia's presence—and her sudden disappearance—hadn't registered. He didn't think Pia even had the chance to hold the baby, with all the medical staff drifting in and out of the room at the time. The disappointment he felt—knowing she'd not only rejected his proposal, but that she couldn't stand being in the same room with him—caused a physical ache in his chest.

He approached the nurses' station, where he was waved into the nursery with a warning to keep quiet. At the exact moment it occurred to him that Pia might have come here, he saw her, leaning over the new prince's bassinet.

Her back was to him, but the nurse beside Pia, more accustomed to the comings and goings of the maternity ward, looked up with interest at his entrance. Unwilling to disturb Pia, he sliced his hand through the air, warning the nurse not to say anything. The nurse nodded her understanding, then focused on Pia. Speaking in San Riminian-accented Italian, she said, "You may hold him, if you wish, Signorina Renati. The princess has given her permission."

"Oh, no," Pia whispered, her own Italian soft and melodic, but her nervousness at such a proposition clear from her stiffening spine. "He looks happy where he is."

The brunette nurse gave Pia a soft smile. "It will be practice for the christening. The princess says that you will be the godmother. And new babies like to be held." The nurse gestured toward a rocking chair in the corner near a row of bassinets, some occupied by sleeping infants. "Sit here. I'll give him to you."

Pia hesitated, then sat, her back still to Federico. "I'm not very good with children."

The nurse tightened the blanket around the wide-eyed baby boy, then placed the burrito-like bundle into

Pia's arms. "Do not worry, signorina. I know he will like you."

"It's not that." Apprehension colored Pia's voice as she looked back down at the little boy in wonder. "I tend to break them."

The nurse dropped into a rocker opposite Pia's. "Not under my observation, you won't. And you are doing fine. See, he is trying to get his arm free, to reach for your finger."

Federico watched a moment longer, as the nurse continued to speak softly to Pia and the baby. Pia gradually sank back against the wooden slats of the rocking chair.

"The pregnancy and parenting books make it all look so easy," he heard Pia comment.

"And the weight loss commercials make it look like anyone can knock off ten kilos without craving cannoli," the nurse deadpanned. "It all takes practice. You'll get there. The baby won't break."

Pia let out a deep breath, but didn't respond.

Without a word, Federico eased back out of the nursery.

"Your Highness, your first interview is in half an hour. The christening is at 11:00 a.m., then I have three more candidates scheduled for this afternoon. Would you care to review their résumés?"

Federico looked up from his desk, where a large stack of correspondence awaited his perusal. He'd been daydreaming again—a luxury he'd rarely afforded himself in the past—but he couldn't get the contradictory images of Pia returning his kisses and Pia walking out on him eradicated from his mind.

He reached out, taking the short stack of résumés and flipping through them. Even if things had gone as he'd hoped with Pia, he'd need to interview new nanny candidates. But somehow, facing yet another group of nervous young women, trying to ascertain who would best care for Arturo and Paolo and what type of influence they'd have on the boys, only served to remind him of Pia's attributes. And of his own failure to convince her to stay.

He'd seen little of Pia in the week since their hospital encounter, but according to Antony, she planned to fly to Africa tonight, after the christening of little Prince Enzo.

"Your Highness? May I help you with something?"

Federico blinked, caught once again staring into space. "I apologize. I have been distracted."

Teodora raised an eyebrow. "I see. If you'd prefer, I'd be happy to do the preliminary interviews for you, to narrow down the field."

He shook his head. "No, I believe we have narrowed it as much as possible already, and I need to make this decision after spending as much time with the candidates as I can." His secretary nodded, retreating to her desk located across the office from his own, but he stopped her as an idea occurred to him. "Teodora, when am I scheduled to complete the interviews today?"

"Around six o'clock, so you will be able to spend the

evening with your sons, if you wish. Princess Isabella offered to take them after the christening, while you conduct the interviews."

He tapped his pen against the desk for a moment. It would be rude, but…

"Is it too late to reschedule this afternoon's interviews for tomorrow? There is something else I need to do, and if it works out, I want the rest of the evening clear." He outlined his plan, then said, "So?"

Teodora's jaw dropped for a fraction of a second before she recovered, nodding as if the request represented nothing out of the ordinary. "Certainly, Your Highness. I—I believe Princess Jennifer has already made the transportation arrangements, however—"

"Call Sophie to rearrange them. But please, do not tell Signorina Renati. I would like to surprise her."

Or, more accurately, keep her from evading him. Before she left forever he would make her face him.

Pia shifted her feet on the aged marble floor, listening without really hearing as the priest told the gathered diTalora family members how Enzo's birth constituted a blessing for both his parents and the country he'd someday rule.

Other than the quiet ministrations of the priest, not a sound could be heard in the Duomo. Even the dust motes of the ancient cathedral had stilled for the ceremony, hanging in midair in the filtered light from the stained glass windows. Though Enzo now stood second in line behind his father to the longest-held throne in

Europe, Jennifer and Antony managed to keep the press out of the service. Only the godparents and immediate family were present, making it the most intimate ceremony the royals had shared in years.

As the priest's words echoed through the cathedral's cavernous gray arches, Pia kept her gaze riveted on the infant. Blissfully asleep in Jennifer's arms, the child wore the same two-hundred-year-old white lace christening gown his father once wore. Every ounce of Pia's energy poured into keeping her eyes turned away from Prince Federico, who stood opposite her before the altar.

She should have known that Jennifer and Antony would ask him to be Enzo's godfather. Antony was closer to Federico than anyone, except his own wife. And that meant, for better or worse, she and Federico would be tied together for life, in at least one small way. Thank goodness there was no godparent rule stating that they had to spend time nurturing the infant together.

Taking a deep breath, Pia tried not to think about Federico's words to her as she had entered the Duomo that morning. Over the rumble of organ music, he'd complimented her on her soft pink dress and choice of heels—both borrowed, of course—and then he'd mentioned that Paolo and Arturo looked forward to eating with her at the palace luncheon planned for after the christening.

He had said that they would miss her when she left, though the way he'd leaned in close to tell her, his warm breath caressing her cheek, his rich baritone making her toes curl inside her high-heeled shoes, left no doubt that he wanted her to know he'd miss her, too.

And that he'd be sitting beside her at the luncheon.

She swallowed back the image of Federico in his immaculate navy-blue suit and raised her eyes to the stunning rose window above his head. Part of her—the logical part—had hoped that he'd forget about her over the course of the week while he went about his royal duties, caring for his children and conducting his search for a new nanny. Twice in the last week she'd seen him on television. Once, at the reopening of a historic home in the heart of the city—soon to be occupied by the American ambassador—and then during a news program where he'd answered a reporter's inquiry by stating that yes, he was scheduling interviews for nanny candidates, and that he hoped whomever he hired might have a positive, lasting influence on his children.

He'd also responded to a rather pointed question about her, replying that yes, Pia Renati was a friend of Jennifer's, and that no, there was no romantic relationship between them.

Hearing him say the words "no romantic relationship" made the part of her that didn't want him to forget about her—the emotional part that dreamed of his kisses and the feel of his large, strong hands cradling her face—ache with emptiness.

As the priest touched the infant's head with holy water, Pia smiled down at Enzo, who looked so tiny and fragile in his gown, and tried to convince herself that she'd made the right choice. During the last week she'd spent enough time watching Jennifer with the baby to start feeling more confident around little Enzo herself, but not enough to care for him without Jennifer or Antony's presence. Despite her desire to help out so the princess might get more sleep, Pia wasn't sure she'd ever be able to stay alone with a baby without being overcome by waves of panic or images of her teenaged accident.

Still, the choice to leave San Rimini—and Federico—hurt her deeply. So deeply that she couldn't look at the prince even now as he stood directly across from her, though she knew by the way her every nerve ending tingled that his blue eyes remained focused on her throughout the ceremony.

Once the organ music began playing again, the king came forward to hug his son and daughter-in-law, and they reviewed plans for returning to the palace for the luncheon. The streets outside the Duomo reverberated with the cheers of thousands of citizens who had all turned out for the chance to glimpse the next generation of the diTalora family, not to mention their king, princes and princesses as they drove along San Rimini's twisting cobblestoned streets.

Pia edged away from Federico to stand behind King Eduardo. Before she could slip out to one of the waiting limousines, however, the king himself stopped her, thanking her for staying with the princess during the last month of her pregnancy. Federico used the opportunity to approach her, and once his father finished speaking, the prince cupped her elbow and propelled her down the main aisle, between the wide rows of pews.

"Ride to the palace with me."

Chapter Nine

Pia slid him a sideways glance. "I thought the plan was for me to ride with Stefano and Amanda, while you—"

He shook his head. "There is a new plan. My father will be riding with Jennifer, Antony and the baby in the lead car. Isabella and Nick will ride with Stef and Amanda. It only makes sense that you ride with me."

In that instant, Pia realized the plans had changed because *Federico* changed them. She tried to school her features to prevent her alarm from showing as Federico spoke. "Besides, it only makes sense that the new godparents ride back to the palace together, *si*?"

"But won't the press think something is up?" She didn't have to add *between the two of us*.

"The boys will ride with us, of course. Nothing could be 'up' with two children at our sides."

Pia gauged her chances of escape, and decided she had little choice. The fact that Amanda, Stefano, Isabella and Nick were already departing through the Duomo's side door to where the limousines waited sealed it.

"All right. I'll ride with you and the boys." She looked around for Paolo and Arturo. They'd been so well-behaved during the service, sitting on a pew just behind their aunts and uncles, she'd forgotten they'd come with the king after she'd arrived.

Federico spotted the boys first, huddled together near the side door, giggling, the jackets on their tiny suits unbuttoned, their shirts partially untucked. The prince walked up behind them, and Pia followed, noticing as she approached that the boys had something hidden in their hands. They jumped when they realized their father stood over them.

"Um, are we ready to go, Papa?" Arturo asked, cupping his hands behind his back.

"Yes. If you show me what you are hiding, first."

"We got hungry," Paolo explained, despite a dirty look from Arturo. "The priest said we could."

"Arturo?" Federico fixed his gaze on his elder son.

Arturo let out a deep sigh, then produced a handful of miniature chocolate bars. "I know we're not supposed to, Papa, but the priest gave them to us and it's going to be forever before we can eat lunch."

Federico extended his hand. "All right. You may each have one more. But I will hold the rest for later."

Grudgingly, Arturo handed over his loot, and Federico tidied the boys' shirts and jackets before steering them out the door to the waiting limousine. Pia barely managed to keep herself from grinning at the boys. Her own stomach rumbled at the sight of the chocolate bars, so how could they expect to wait two hours past their normal lunchtime to be fed?

Thankfully the ride would take only a few minutes, assuming the San Riminian police managed to keep the crowd back behind the metal barriers, and she'd be able to nibble on appetizers while circulating amongst the members of parliament and the aristocracy gathering for the celebratory lunch.

The preluncheon cocktail hour also afforded her the opportunity to slip away from Federico. As he handed her into the limousine, then slid into the seat beside her, she fought the urge to slide closer to him, to reach out and put her hand on his knee, and to tell him that yes, she'd made a terrible mistake, and she'd love to stay and see if they could make a relationship work.

How could one man possess so much charisma? The very air in the limousine seemed charged with his presence. Thank goodness the luncheon would be hosted in the palace's spacious Imperial Ballroom.

"I understand you are scheduled to leave for Africa tonight," Federico said as the driver revved the engine, then pulled away from the Duomo to follow the limousine carrying the king.

At Pia's nod, he encouraged the boys to go ahead and open their candy, then lowered his voice. "I realize that this is not the time or place, but I must speak with you before you go. I—I saw you in the nursery, the day Enzo was born. I walked in behind you, and I left before you could see me. I know I should have announced my presence, but I did not wish to interrupt." He drew a deep breath, and Pia turned to face him, instantly realizing what he must have overheard. She'd never wanted him to know the depth of her fears, especially since he had allowed her to play with his own two children, but maybe it was for the best. Maybe now he'd let her go.

"Pia, why did you tell the nurse—"

As high a stake as she had in the prince's words, a sudden noise from Paolo made her turn her attention toward the little boy, who sat beside Arturo on the bench seat directly opposite the seat she and Federico occupied. "Paolo? Paolo, are you all right?"

Before her eyes Paolo's face went crimson, first his cheeks, then from the top of his head down to his throat. He sputtered, attempting to cough but failing. Panicked, he fixed his gaze on her, soundlessly pleading for help.

"He's choking," she managed, even as she unbuckled her seat belt and knelt in front of the boy. As rapidly as she could she freed him from his booster seat, leaned him forward into her arms, and pounded him on the back a few times. The wrapper of his candy bar remained clutched in his hand.

Pia worked quickly, loosening his tie, then unbuttoning the top of his shirt. She leaned him forward and tried once more to dislodge the candy.

Federico knelt on the limousine floor beside Pia.

"Paolo, oh no, Paolo…" He leaned over the children's seat, catching the driver's eye in the rearview mirror. "Pull over, immediately," he commanded. "And call for an ambulance."

"Your Highness, if we pull over here, we would be mobbed," the driver tilted his head toward the crowd lining the side of the cobblestoned street. "And with the street blocked off, an ambulance will have difficulty getting through. I recommend we pass your father's car and get to the palace." Without waiting for Federico's agreement, he snatched up the cell phone mounted to the dash and called ahead, telling whoever answered to have the doctor waiting by the palace's front doors.

In the meantime Pia grabbed Paolo around the waist, wedging him into her lap as best she could in the confined space between the two facing bench seats. With Paolo no longer able to breathe, Pia had no intention of waiting until they arrived at the palace to help him.

"Paolo," she instructed, fighting to keep her voice firm as she hoisted him so his head was just in front of hers. "I'm going to put my hands under your ribs, here." She made a double fist with her hands, then found the tiny space at the base of his rib cage. "Just try to go limp against me, okay?"

The little boy kept fighting, his instincts sending him scurrying toward his father. Arturo cried out for his brother, terror edging his voice, but understanding what Pia needed, Federico ignored Arturo and crouched in front of Paolo, encouraging him to listen to Pia. For just a moment, Paolo met his father's eyes and his body relaxed. Pia thrust her hands up and in, then again, then again.

C'mon, Paolo, c'mon. Paolo's utter silence and his darkening face sent fingers of panic through Pia's heart. She forced back the vision of a little girl's hair sailing over her head as she went flying through the air....

With an internal prayer she tried a fourth time to eject the candy from Paolo's throat, and nearly cried when a half-melted piece of chocolate shot out of the little boy's mouth, landing on his father's pristine navy trousers, then sliding down to the limousine's carpeted floor.

Paolo crumpled against her, sucking in lungfuls of air as a cry ripped from his throat.

At once, Federico enclosed both of them in a hug. "All right, Paolo. You will be all right now, no need for tears. *Tutto va bene.*"

Pia dropped her head down on top of Paolo's, relief flooding through her. What would she have done had Paolo been unable to cough up the candy? Would they have made it to the palace? How would Federico have handled such devastation?

"You scared me, Paolo," she whispered against his soft brown hair, cradling him to her.

"Me, too," Federico murmured.

"Me, too!" Arturo cried, launching himself from his seat and clutching at Federico's broad shoulders.

Pia shook her head, then reluctantly eased back from Federico's strong embrace. Now that the danger had passed, the part of her that fought against getting any closer to Federico or his family emerged.

Sitting on the floor of the car, even as the driver lurched along the cobblestoned streets at a breakneck pace to return to the palace, felt entirely too good. And being hugged by Federico and the boys felt too…too *right*. As if she'd finally found the loving family she'd wanted so badly as a child.

"Let's get you back in your car seat," she told Paolo as the limousine careened around another corner, "before there's another accident."

Paolo nodded, his face still registering shock from the episode. Silently, he climbed back into his seat. Federico leaned past her to tell the driver all was well and that he could slow down. As Pia buckled Paolo's safety belt and Arturo clambered back onto his own booster seat, Federico's hand warmed her shoulder.

"*Grazie mille,* Pia. I have never assisted a choking victim before, let alone my own son. I am not sure I could have—"

"*I'm* sure. You would have." Pia sat back on her own seat, and a glance out the window surprised her with a view of the palace's impressive facade. "I've never done anything like that before, either. And if you'd asked me, even with all the first aid training I received for my job, I would never claim to be confident I could handle a real-life situation."

"You should be confident." Federico's tone was pointed, reminding her he'd overheard her nursery conversation. Glancing at Paolo, and seeing his color returning to normal, she conceded that Federico had a point. Perhaps she wasn't as incapable as she'd always feared herself to be. Especially where a small child was concerned.

As they rolled to a stop at the palace's grand front entrance, reporters and cameramen who'd been afforded exclusive access to the palace grounds for the christening of San Rimini's future king surged toward the vehicle. All of them yelled the same questions through the car windows—why had the occupants of the limousine been spotted on the floor? Why had they surged ahead of the procession? Was there an emergency of some sort?

Federico allowed his driver to open the car door, assuring the reporters he'd answer their questions momentarily. He reached back in to help Pia from the car, and at the blast of camera flashes exploding in her face, she reflexively gripped Federico's hand tighter than appropriate.

Once Federico unbuckled the boys, he handed them off to his secretary and the palace doctor, who'd pushed their way through the crowd. Federico leaned in to speak in Teodora's ear, quietly telling her what happened in the car and asking her to have the doctor check Paolo over before she took the boys to the reception.

Once both boys had been safely escorted inside, Federico eased Pia toward the palace steps, then turned to respond to the reporters' questions.

As Pia stood on the lowest step, within arm's reach of the journalists gathered on the expansive front walk, a feeling of déjà vu gripped her. The sea of reporters mirrored the scene at the hospital just after she'd received her stitches. And her emotions concerning Federico were even stronger now, and more confused, than they were on that day, when he'd given her that first searing, knee-weakening kiss.

"Your Highness—"

Federico raised his hands to quiet the buzz of the crowd. "In answer to your questions, we had a slight scare in the car. Nothing to worry about. I allowed Paolo to have some candy as we drove back here from the Duomo, and he decided it might be interesting to see what would happen if he swallowed it whole."

A few of the reporters smiled in response to Federico's lighthearted tone, though by their expressions, none seemed ready to accept such a simple explanation. Federico quickly added, "Thanks to Signorina Renati, nothing serious happened. Paolo, as you saw when we arrived, is just fine. A little choked up over his cousin's christening, perhaps," he joked, "but fine."

Pia backed up the staircase away from the journalists as they fired off a barrage of follow-up questions.

"What exactly did Signorina Renati do?"

"Is she qualified to treat a member of the royal family?"

"How can you be certain the prince is well?"

"How serious was the incident, really? Could Prince Paolo breathe?"

"Was the prince—"

Federico tried to speak over the noise, assuring them that Paolo was never in any real danger, but before the reporters could push him for more detail, the limousine carrying King Eduardo, the Crown Prince and Princess, and Prince Enzo pulled into the circular drive. The new arrival distracted most of the reporters, all of whom had been sent to the palace with the sole mission of getting the first photographs of the new diTalora infant.

"Follow me." Federico nudged Pia, and she turned and strode up the stairs after him, making the most of the opportunity to escape. Within seconds they passed through the palace's doors and were surrounded by staff, who blocked the reporters' view of the palace interior and stood ready to take the coats of guests who were scheduled to arrive behind the motorcade from the Duomo.

Pia grinned at Federico as he led her down the wide entrance hall toward the Imperial Ballroom. "I was wondering how long they'd grill us before we could break for lunch. I'm starved."

Federico didn't respond. Instead, once they were out of sight of the staff, in the rotunda just outside the Imperial Ballroom, he grabbed her hand and pulled her down with him onto a large upholstered sofa beneath a floor-to-ceiling window that opened onto the palace gardens.

"Federico?"

"You are not getting away so easily. From me, or from the conversation we started in the car."

Pia glanced back down the hall. The rest of the royal family hadn't yet entered the palace, and she had to assume the reporters would occupy them for some time. "Listen, Federico—"

"What is it about children that terrifies you? And why are you using it as an excuse to leave, when you know we are meant to be together?"

Pia coughed, fighting the urge to stand and run. He'd progressed from "stay and give it a try" to "meant to be together," despite the fact that she'd deliberately stayed away from him?

"Well, for someone who's spent his whole life acting the perfect royal, you sure can be blunt when you want to be."

"Pia—"

"Okay, okay." She worried her lip, and tried not to think about the fact that he still had her hand trapped in his. "It's not that children terrify me, exactly. I don't think I should be taking care of them, that's all. It's not Arturo and Paolo—it's all children, which is why I can't stay with you. I'm just not the sort of person you can trust them with."

"A person who's caring, intelligent and loving? A person who I told—and I meant what I said—would make a wonderful mother someday? I have seen you caring for Jennifer. You took time away from your job to do so—a job I know you value as much as I do mine, making life better for hundreds of people. And I've seen you with my sons." He tightened his left hand around hers, and cupped her chin with his right, forcing her to look straight into his sharp blue eyes. "I dare you, right now, to deny that you are all those things. Stay. Or go, if you must. But do not use your fears as an excuse."

Tears tightened her throat before welling up in her eyes. She *wasn't* any of those things—certainly she was not mother material. She'd enjoyed her time with Paolo and Arturo, but in her heart she knew that she'd simply been trying to fill the hours while Jennifer recovered. And trying to get Federico out of her system.

Since she'd failed miserably on that count, the thought of staying…while it was certainly tempting, and no woman in her right mind could turn her back on such a devastating man, she knew her fears were real. Not some imagined excuse.

The boys didn't deserve that. And Federico didn't deserve it, either. He deserved a devoted, loving wife. Someone who craved the royal life as Lucrezia did, but who saw him for the fascinating man he was and appreciated each facet of his layered, complex personality. Who loved him as he deserved to be loved.

He thought he loved her. But how could he, when he didn't realize the difference between the woman he saw and the woman she knew herself to be?

She shook her head. "It's no excuse. Believe me, Federico, going to Africa is the right thing for me to do."

"Why do you doubt yourself?" His eyes were shrewd, assessing, and concern tinged his speech. "Are you…are you unable to conceive? Is this why you are so sensitive to—"

"No, that's not it. I mean, I don't know. It's not the kind of thing you usually discover unless you're in the situation."

He massaged the back of her hand with his thumb, his voice comforting as he spoke. "I am sorry. I had to ask. But then, what is it about children that disturbs you? In the nursery, when Enzo was born, I overheard you tell the nurse that you feared you might break him. I cannot imagine you doing such a thing, yet your apprehension was obvious. So—?"

His gentle expression showed so much love, so much worry, that she had to tell him. Had to take the chance he'd understand and let her go, knowing she wasn't the best thing for him, no matter how strong his feelings for her—or hers for him.

She eased her hand from his. "You've probably figured out that I don't get along with my mother so well."

Surprise flickered in his eyes. Apparently not the reason he'd expected her to give. "I did wonder. You were not comfortable talking about her at breakfast last week, the day we took the boys out in the rain."

Pia nodded. "My mother's a great person, really. I'm finally beginning to appreciate her. But when I was young, she wasn't around much, so she wasn't exactly the kind of mom I could emulate."

She let out a halfhearted laugh. "When I was sixteen, I couldn't stand her. That's about the same time I got my very first job, babysitting a neighbor's kid. A little girl about Arturo's age."

As if knowing what she'd say next, he shifted closer to her on the sofa, moving a loose pillow out of the way. "What happened?"

"Long story short, the little girl fell backward out of

a swing. I pushed her too high, and she broke her collarbone and did damage to her kidneys from landing so hard." She closed her eyes for a moment, wishing never to imagine the little girl's stricken, pained look again. When met with Federico's concerned gaze again, she explained, "I felt horrible, but much, much worse when I tried to describe what happened to the girl's father. He yelled at me like you wouldn't believe. He was this huge guy, really muscular and kind of scary, at least to me, even though he'd never been anything but kind to me before that day. When I finished telling him everything he said I couldn't be trusted, that he never should have hired a girl whose own mother couldn't take care of her."

Pia screwed up her mouth at Federico's sickened look. "I know, I know. I shouldn't have believed him. He was under a lot of stress, accidents happen, he didn't mean what he said and all that. But deep down, I did believe him. I knew what he said about my mother was true, and he wasn't the only one to say it."

"But because of him, you believe that you cannot stay with me because of Arturo and Paolo? Do you truly believe you would harm them?"

Pia pressed her fingers to the base of her eye sockets in an attempt to hold in her tears. "I'd never harm them. Not knowingly. But I have a lot of doubts. They might not be rational, but I care so much about you, Federico. I think I might even be in love with you." She bit down on her lower lip, knowing it was stupid to have told him, yet unable to stop the words. "Enough not to put your sons at risk. And enough to know there are literally millions of women in the world who would kill to be with you—intelligent, beautiful women without my stupid doubts."

To her amazement, Federico's quiet laugh echoed through the empty rotunda.

"Pia." Easing her fingers away from her face, he smiled and shook his head. "What if I told you we have much in common. After my experience with Lucrezia, I doubted myself—I daresay as much as your experience made you question yourself. I was certain I would never know love for a woman—that I would mistake comfort for love, or that I was simply incapable of it. You were certain you could never care for children— that you were incapable of keeping them from harm."

"You make us sound so pathetic," she returned his amused grin. "How could you possibly argue that we'd be good together?"

"Because we are both working to overcome our doubts. When I met you, I finally understood that a woman could not only make me feel intense emotion, but could also make me a better father to my children. And you are learning that you can care for children without something terrible coming to pass."

Sarcasm edged her laugh. "Yeah. What happened to Paolo just now? That wasn't so terrible."

"Because you were there to help. And it was not your fault it happened in the first place. *I* was the one who permitted him to eat candy in the car, then did not watch closely as he did so."

"But it doesn't matter, does it? Kids are so unpredictable. You never know when an emergency might arise. And even though I managed in the car with Paolo, look what happened when he went running in the fountain. I panicked. And when Arturo jumped out of that swing, I couldn't even move to help, I was so scared, I was useless to—"

Noise from the palace entrance floated into the rotunda. causing both Pia and Federico to turn on the sofa. King Eduardo's voice stood out from the crowd, and Pia realized the guests were arriving.

"Listen," she began, "we really don't have much time to discuss this. Bottom line is, you can do better than a shrimpy blonde who goes into insta-panic mode whenever she sees a kid do the things kids normally do. I care for you enough to want the best for you, and for your sons."

The creases across Federico's brow deepened, and he shook his head. "*You* are what is best for me, and for the boys. Do you not understand? You are stronger than you think. What happened with Arturo *should* have scared you—he was on a *swing,* of all things. But he wasn't in any real danger. I think part of you knew that. Then, when Paolo played his prank in the fountain, you *did* react. You pulled him out of the water, even though you knew he had to be all right. I saw the entire event. Paolo was only away from your side for three or four seconds. Not long enough for harm to have come to him."

"Still—"

"Still, the one time it counted—when Paolo was choking—you acted as any doctor might. You were calm, you removed him from his car seat, and you saved his life."

Federico glanced past her, toward the sound of his father and Antony's voices, which were moving closer.

Pia pulled away from the prince and stood, trying not to feel wobbly in her unfamiliar high heels. "I'm glad Paolo's all right, and not just because of the confidence boost it gives me. But Federico, I can't be expected to get over a lifetime of misgivings—as irrational as they might be—in a single day."

"So stay." He rose beside her, then caressed her cheeks, forcing her to look him in the eye as he spoke. In a whisper, he pleaded, "Stay. Take the time to discover your capabilities. And to discover what we have."

Pia tried not to breathe, knowing that even a hint of his warm, clean scent filling her nostrils would send her over the edge, though his hands and his gaze alone threatened to do it.

"What about my job?" she asked slowly. "I can't just walk away. People are counting on me."

Federico's mouth quirked, as if the mere question showed she might crack. "Talk to Jennifer about your options. She no longer spends her days in dirty, isolated camps helping refugees, but she is making a real difference with her charity work. You could, too. Your experience in the world, spending time in isolated locations in a way someone with my position never can, will make all the difference in your ability to raise awareness about a cause. Just think what would happen if you could use the resources of the royal palace to make the world realize the extent of the AIDS epidemic in Africa."

He sighed, letting his hands fall to her shoulders. "If you need to finish the job you committed to in Africa, I understand. But I fear if you go, you might not return. And I fear you will begin to question yourself again, and you will use the job to hide from your problems."

Pia pulled back, stunned. Had she used her job to hide? She'd used it to escape her mother, of course. When she'd graduated college and faced returning to San Rimini to seek employment, she'd jumped on the chance not only to help people, but to stay far away from Sabrina. But had the job also been an excuse to escape *life?* Her friends graduated and started families, while for someone in her profession, pursuing a romance posed a great challenge—and that meant little risk of children.

She tried to swallow against the emotion clogging her throat. "How is it that you know more about me than I do?" Never in a million years would she have guessed the proper prince would understand her. But he did. Better than she understood herself.

He ran a finger along the collar of her dress and smiled. "Because we have much in common. Your job is an escape for you. And I now realize mine has served the same role."

At her confused frown, he continued, "I told you at the hospital that I never loved Lucrezia. When I proposed to her, I believed it was for the right reasons. One must only look at the Windsors to understand how I convinced myself that marrying Lucrezia—a friend who would never embarrass me, and who was willing to become a textbook princess—was the logical thing to do. But the truth is, I feared for my own reputation. I saw what the press did to Antony before he married Jennifer, referring to him as a playboy. I also knew my father would never question my decision. Lucrezia was intelligent, very beautiful and from a good family."

"But—?"

"We understood each other, and I called it love. It was not. It was comfortable. I used my position to justify my decision, but in truth, I married Lucrezia to escape any chance my romantic life might become tabloid material. I did not believe love was worth ruining my reputation."

He shook his head, and Pia realized how he strained to contain his own emotions. "It took losing Lucrezia—and finding you—to realize how rewarding, how *amazing* love can be. Now that I have discovered it, I do not wish to let it go. I do not wish to let you go."

"Even if it means you might sacrifice your reputation? You yourself said you wanted to honor Lucrezia. If I stay—even if we take things very slowly—you know what the press will say. And the citizens of San Rimini."

"What if I told you I am willing to take the chance?"

A laugh escaped her. "You really shouldn't—"

"Yes, I should. And I will. Just agree to stay."

At that moment the rest of the royal family entered the rotunda and headed for the Imperial Ballroom. Guests surrounded the king and his children, all vying for a chance to see Prince Enzo and to be seen with the diTaloras. Flashbulbs popped and men with video cameras wove in and out of the group, capturing the event for the evening news. It only took a few seconds for the reporters to spot Federico standing close to Pia, and to turn their cameras toward the couple, hoping for a scoop.

Pia smiled at the prince and, feeling like a cliff diver about to take a dangerous leap into unknown waters, she nodded.

Federico's face split into a wide grin just before he leaned forward and kissed her.

Cameramen surrounded them, snapping away, and Pia laughed against Federico's lips. Yes, she owed herself this chance.

"I don't believe I shall be called 'Prince Perfect' any longer," he whispered for her ears only, his words barely audible over the shocked conversation surrounding them.

"You're wrong," she replied, kissing him. "You're *my* Prince Perfect. And I plan to remind you every day."

Epilogue

Three Years Later

"I still don't think I know a placenta previa from a placenta accereta," Pia whispered to Federico, careful to keep Arturo and Paolo from hearing her as she stood behind them at their nursery table and helped Arturo with his school project.

"I do not think it will matter." Federico lightly touched his hand to her lower back, then leaned forward to brush the top of her head with a kiss. "And if it does, we will learn together."

"Mamma, you told me it is not polite to whisper," Paolo frowned at her.

"You're right. I'm setting a bad example." She

winked at Paolo, who now reminded her so much of Arturo when she'd first met them on the day they'd struck her with the boomerang. Paolo had grown into a confident, bright little first grader.

And she couldn't be more thrilled that both boys had started to call her Mamma.

"I think your mother is setting a very good example," Federico said as he picked up the piece of paper Arturo finished working on. "The children at the AIDS shelter in Zimbabwe will be very excited to receive all the letters from you and your classmates."

"And my pictures," Paolo added, holding up a watercolor painting that Pia guessed was of Paolo himself. "Will we get to go visit them again soon?"

Pia and Federico's gazes met, and a secretive smile passed between them. "Mamma might not be able to travel to Africa for a while, Paolo," Federico said. "She is working on a very important project of her own."

"What kind of project?" Arturo straightened in his chair and set down his pencil. "Is it for the children?"

Pia grinned, thinking of the gift Federico had given her the night before—a yellow, floral-jacketed pregnancy book, and a brand-spanking new copy of *The Ultra-Hip Mom's Guide To Baby's First Year,* third edition. "It has to do with children, yes, but—"

"But it's a secret for now," Federico finished. "We shall tell you more about Mamma's project later, all right? For now, we should clean up this mess. Your new nanny will arrive at any moment to take you to the movies."

"You *finally* found a nanny, Papa?" Paolo asked. "Mamma said she didn't think you'd ever find one."

"I didn't," Pia admitted. "But I found someone who just retired, and she tells me that all her life she's wanted nothing more than to care for children. Now she has the chance."

Arturo's eyes brightened. "It's Grandma Sabrina, isn't it?"

Pia couldn't help but grin in response. "Clean up quick, or you'll never know, will you?"

"It is! It is!" Both boys cheered and gave each other high fives. Then, as they scrambled to clean up the mess, Federico leaned in close to Pia and whispered, "Once they leave, we shall celebrate in private."

"We're supposed to be attending Nick and Isabella's fundraiser for the Royal Museum of San Rimini's medieval art exhibit."

"So we'll be late." He grinned.

"You can't get me—you know—when I'm already—"

"It would be fun to try, though."

She raised an eyebrow, then skirted the table to help the boys tidy their art projects. "If you insist, Your Highness. It's not as if I can escape."

"No," he assured her, reaching across the table to hold her hand and run his fingers over her gold wedding band. "You can't."

* * * * *

SILHOUETTE *Romance*®

Coming September 2004 from

KAREN ROSE SMITH

Once Upon a Baby...
(Silhouette Romance #1737)

Marriage was the last thing on eternal bachelor Simon Blackstone's mind when he offered to help the very beautiful—and very pregnant—Risa Parker. But the closer Simon gets to the glowing mother-to-be, the closer he'll come to wanting to claim Risa and her baby as his own....

Available at your favorite retail outlet.

If you enjoyed what you just read,
then we've got an offer you can't resist!

Take 2 bestselling
love stories FREE!
Plus get a FREE surprise gift!

SILHOUETTE *Romance* ®

They're back!

THE BRUBAKER BRIDES

The Brubaker sisters are on the loose and they're fixin' to make themselves the next batch of BRUBAKER BRIDES.

Carolina's Gone A'Courting

(Silhouette Romance #1734)

by **CAROLYN ZANE**

Hunter Crenshaw got more than he bargained for when spitfire Carolina Brubaker crashed into his life. She was infuriating, exasperating…and unbelievably attractive. Before Hunt knew what hit him, Carolina had set him on a collision course with destiny.

Available September 2004 at your favorite retail outlet.